RIVER HAWKS RUN

River Hawks Run

JIM FERGUSON

Ridgecroft Media

Eric and Mikayla,

thank you for letting me tell my stories.

| 1 |

It was just past the two-mile mark, at the crest of the cross country course's final hill, when Drew Declan saw the lead pack had broken up and the runners stretched out single file ahead of him. Everything had gone to plan: he didn't get sucked out too fast with the early leaders, yet had run hard enough to put himself ahead of the rest of the field. Entering the last mile he felt strong enough to pick up the pace and knock off as many runners as he could. Each runner he passed would lower his score. Now, in the last cross country race of his high school career, he was determined to turn it up, fight the pain, and run as hard as he possibly could.

The lousy weather, gray, raw, and cold with rain showers, fired him up even more. Chasing down runners while battling the elements made it tougher, more painful, and fun. Every runner he passed was one more kid who he was better than. This was competition in its purest form: start a race and see who had the speed, the strength, and the guts to get to the finish first.

He wasn't sure how far back from the leader he was, but he felt that he must be in the top thirty. He had won most of his team's dual meets this season, but in a statewide race like this, he just wanted to run a good time and score as few points. The River Hawks had only four guys qualify for the race, so they didn't have a complete team. There would be no team score. This race was all about testing himself. How fast could he go? How many people could he beat?

There were no spectators on the backside of the hill. The only sounds on the deserted golf course were the runner's footfalls landing on the hard-packed grass. The race course had covered different types of terrain, soft grass of the fairways, gravel on an old parking lot, bark mulch near the start line, and each surface had its own distinct sound of pounding feet. At one point the runners briefly ran over a concrete walkway and Drew heard some runner's shoes make a "click-click" sound on the hard surface. *They must be wearing spikes,* he thought. The sprinters on the outdoor team used spikes, but it had never occurred to him to wear them for XC.

Drew's best distance was the mile, not the 5K, and in all the track races he had run, he had never worn spikes. Maybe if he dropped down to the 880 he would have worn a pair, but in XC? Never thought of it.

At first he was worried. Will the other runners have an advantage over him? The conditions on the course were lousy. The rain made the grass slippery and there were plenty of spots with slick mud. Running at this speed, especially late in the race when legs are tired, one poor foot placement could send him sprawling to the ground and ruin his race.

Then his worry turned to anger. He should have thought of spiked shoes. He had heard of some kids starting to wear spikes for XC, but had dismissed as a fad. If those spiked shoes do give the others an advantage over him, he would be so mad at him-self for not being prepared.

Anger turned into resolve. He was not going to let any spiked-shoed suburban kid beat him in this race. The sixty mile weeks he ran over the summer made his legs strong. Twice-a-week track workouts during the season gave his legs speed and sharpness. He had weeks of training without injury, and he was fit. He saw weakness in the runners in front of him and spikes or no spikes, he was going to push his body forward and pass them all.

Into the last half mile he pushed his pace, passing one runner, then another. The rain started to fall again making his River Hawks singlet cling to his chest. Despite the low temperature, his body's core had built up plenty of heat and felt warm, but his thin arms were cold and fingers were freezing. His breathing became louder and deeper, grunting with every exhale. His legs, splattered with grass stains and mud up to the knees, were still strong and churned over the turf.

The pain of exertion grew and his body begged to slow down. Being a runner—a real runner—he knew that when a race became most painful, it was the time to push himself even more. His thoughts narrowed and his mind focused on keeping the pace. He didn't think of teammates, his coach, the rain, or even spiked shoes anymore. One pervasive, singular train of thought filled his mind: keep on going. Push the pace. Fight the pain. Pass the next guy.

A few spectators lined the trail closer to the finish. Some were shouting to a specific runner ahead or behind him. Some gave a generic cheer to any runner going by at the moment.

Their words were unintelligible to Drew, incapable of penetrating the mental focus this stage of the race required. Yet there was a phrase that broke through. One spectator's yell was unlike the others and its uniqueness begged to be listened to. The words didn't make sense, and at first didn't seem like words at all but rather some kind of rhythmic chanting, "... doce... trece... catorce..."

Drew tried to solve the problem. It had been a man's voice, not another student. He was older—probably someone's dad who had taken the afternoon off to watch the race. The words weren't English, but Spanish. Finally it became apparent. The man had been counting. He was letting the runners know what place they were in the race.

Drew had taken Spanish his freshman and sophomore years and hated it. He did well in math, history, and science classes, but Spanish had been his worst subject. His parents even had to pay for a tutor so he could maintain a C average and stay eligible to run. The last day in Mrs. Ramirez's classroom was the last time he had spoken a word of Spanish, and whatever he had learned had long since left his mind. *What was doce, trece, catorce,* he thought?

The race churned on and Drew passed another weaker runner. It was exhausting work. His exhales became louder with the strain. Why was he wasting his focus on Spanish? *Focus on the race,* he reprimanded himself. And then it hit him: "doce, trece, catorce" was "twelve, thirteen, fourteen." He had just moved into thirteenth place!

Three hundred and fifty of the best high school runners in the state started this race, and now, with a quarter mile to go,

Drew Declan of Aiken was in the top fifteen. The fact shocked him. He knew he was a good miler, but he had always doubted his ability to hang with the best over the longer distance of a cross country race. His coach, Mr. Morrissey, pegged him as a runner fast enough to compete with the top runners, but Drew didn't have the confidence in himself to believe it. And yet there he was.

The jolt of confidence made him reevaluate his position in his athletic life. He really did belong with the top runners in the state. He was a stronger runner than just about all of them. This was his sport, and he was one of the best.

Click-click. The race course crossed a cement walkway again and Drew heard the shoes of the two runners ahead of him. *Damn, spike wearers,* he thought. They were in eleventh and twelfth place. He looked at the body language of the two runners and liked what he saw. The runner closest to him was running at good speed but his arms were swinging too far from his body. *That guy has no upper body strength,* thought Drew dismissively. He knew he had more strength for the final kick than him.

The eleventh place runner's head was tilted back, chin pointing up. *He's toast,* thought Drew, realizing he would easily pass both. The real question was how far ahead was the tenth place runner?

Oh my god, thought Drew. A top ten finish in the state meet was possible. He could be one of the best runners in the state. No one in his school—no football players, no basketball players, no one from the soccer or baseball teams—could say they were in the top ten in their sport. It would be Drew alone at the top of the entire high school athletic pyramid.

The eleventh and twelfth place runners didn't put up much resistance, and entering the final hundred yards of the race, Drew closed in on Runner Ten. The crowds were thicker now, maybe two or three deep behind the bright orange plastic fences that lined the chute for the final yards. And they were loud. They saw a close finish coming up between Drew and Runner Ten.

Runner Ten, tall and thin with curly red hair that flopped in the wind, was struggling to hold his place in the race. Hearing the excitement in the crowd, he turned to look back over his shoulder. His eyes went wide with shock as he saw Drew bearing down on him, just five yards behind.

When Drew saw the look on Runner Ten's face he knew any element of surprise was over and Runner Ten would try to kick it in. Drew had to give every bit of energy he had left right now.

He bared down and turned up his leg turnover. His increased speed closed the gap, but Runner Ten had also sped up in his last desperate kick to keep ahead of Drew. With about twenty yards to go they were side by side, each doing their best version of a sprint after racing for more than three miles.

For Drew it was more than three miles. It had been four years of cross country and track. It had been finding a sport that he was good at and loved. It was realizing he was better than the other guys at something. It was about getting faster and better every year. It was about summer-long build up of distance, hard tempo runs, and killer track workouts. It was about learning that hard work, persistence, and dedication made you stronger and faster. And right at that moment, it was about digging a little deeper, dealing with a little more pain, and moving your body a little faster than the next guy.

Five yards to go, still side by side, Drew heard Runner Ten gasp, "Ugh." The kid had maxed out and couldn't keep the pace. Runner Ten pitched his shoulders forward and started to lose his balance - his legs just couldn't hold him up anymore. Drew took two more strides, leaned his chest forward, and crossed the finish line as the tenth fastest runner in the state.

The instant relief from pain washed over Drew's body. He wobbled to a stop, his chest heaving with each breath. The blood pressure dropped in his body and, feeling dizzy, he bent down and put his hands on his knees to steady himself. Runner Ten (actually, now runner eleven) was splayed out in the mud a few feet beyond the finish line. The meet officials were trying to get him up and out of the way of other runners entering the chute. Runners twelve and thirteen crossed the line, their bodies withered, weak and spent from the total exertion.

With his breathing coming under control, Drew raised his head and surveyed the scene. The runners' bodies, splattered with dirt and drenched with rain, were strewn on the grass and mud of the recovery area. Many of them, their legs were sapped of normal strength, tottered out of balance as they walked. Some drank from water bottles. Some reached out to shake the hand of a close competitor. A few doubled over and wretched out the remaining fluid from their stomachs on the patch of grass between their shoes.

It was a scene that most people would hate to find themselves in. Non-runners recoil at the number of miles, the exertion, and the physical demands of racing. Even the guys on the other teams, the football players or soccer players, dread running more than twenty yards at a time. It took a special mindset to willingly push your body and suffer the pain. For Drew, running fast brought joy.

The success of his race flooded Drew's body with endorphins. Years of training and hard work had culminated in a race that made him one of the best. He survived the rain, mud, and the pain, and had run his best race. He had succeeded beyond his wildest dreams. This was his sport and he was one of the best.

He smiled, tilted his head back to the gray sky above, and declared out loud, "My God, I love this!"

| 2 |

In the two-week gap between the end of the fall high school sports season and the beginning of the winter season, athletes in Aiken High rested, regrouped, and looked forward to their next sport. Even though Drew liked cross country and was coming off his best race, it was racing the mile for indoor track that he liked the most. He had been looking forward to and preparing for this season since last March.

Unlike fall cross country, which required only seven varsity members, all of whom were distance runners, a successful indoor team called for many athletes who varied in speed and strength. From sprints to shot put, a track team was a collection of individuals all pulling in their own direction. Drew knew there were plenty of good athletes across Aiken High, and it was so clear to him that if he could get the right guys in the right events, the River Hawks would have a powerful team. They just needed someone to make them all pull together. The only problem was that most of the athletes in his school didn't care about track.

The popular sports at school, like basketball or hockey, were where the best athletes gravitated. Those teams had tryouts where a surplus of athletes competed just to be a member of the team. Not track. There were no tryouts. No one was cut. The group of kids that showed up at the beginning of the season was the team. Runners would join and drop off as the season wore on, and no one, not even Coach Morrissey, seemed to mind. The structure and discipline of the team was, to say the least, loose, and it showed in their dismal win-loss record. Through his first three years at Aiken High the indoor team never had a winning record.

Drew wanted something different for his senior year. Running and winning his races in the mile was fun, but he desired more than just individual reward. He saw himself leading the entire team to victory. He was positive that the guys in his school were good enough to be winners. As the only senior on the XC team, and the de facto leader of the boys indoor team, he figured it was up to him to recruit athletes from the fall and spring sports. Guys who might want to take the winter off from the team sports but still stay in shape would be perfect for indoor. They just needed some convincing. Old Mr. Morrissey wasn't going to go around and find the guys with talent, but Drew would.

Before he started recruiting the likes of spring baseball players to run during the winter, Drew had to make sure the core runners from cross country were on board.

The number two, three and four runners on the XC team were the only distance guys who had the dedication and talent to be relied upon to score points for the River Hawks. Gil and Casey, both juniors, logged a lot of miles this fall, and were strong distance runners. No one else at Aiken High could come close to them in the two mile. Tooch, just a sophomore, would follow Drew in the mile. Drew may be able to find a soccer player willing to race a sprint or middle distance race, but he had never come across one who would voluntarily run the high mileage needed to be a strong distance runner. When it came to scoring points in the mile and two mile, these guys were irreplaceable.

The time they spent together on their long runs had made them friends. They were quiet kids when around a large group or walking in the school hallways, but when safely in the pack of distance runners they were constantly talking, arguing, debating, correcting, and most of all, making fun of each other. Their success at running was their common bond. Gil and Tooch were new to the country and both spoke English as their second language. Gil spent the first years of his life in Brazil. Tooch's entire family came from Cambodia. Casey, blond, blue eyed, and much taller than the other two, took a different bus home from school to the affluent Beech Hill Estates. They grew up in three parts of the world, and now ran together in Aiken.

There were no official practices between seasons, but the four runners still met after school to run a few easy miles.

"All right, guys, let's lay out your goals for the indoor season," said Drew. They were a little more than a mile into the run and all the talk so far had been about last week's state XC race.

"Goals? You have goals for us?" laughed Casey. He liked to tease Drew and his grandiose plans. "Like a guidance counselor for sports? Are you going to mail grades to all our parents?"

"Of course he has goals," corrected Gil. "He's probably been devising them for months."

Drew ignored the chatter and pressed on. "One of you two will win every regular season race," he said, "and in the state meet you push each other to place."

"Every meet?" questioned Gil. He never let an incorrect statement go by without challenging it. There was bound to be a faster runner from another town in one of their dual meets.

"The states aren't till the beginning of March," complained Casey. It seemed crazy to be thinking that far ahead. "Besides," he joked, "how can I push him if he is always behind me?"

"You've never led a race in your life," retorted Gil.

Team scoring for regular season meets in indoor was simple. The first finisher in each race received five points for his team, the second runner received three points and third place one. The two indoor field events, shot put and high jump, scored the same way. Drew figured he was a five-pointer in the mile, and Tooch, maybe a one-pointer. Depending on who was having a better day racing the two mile Gil could be a five-pointer and Casey a three-pointer, or the other way around.

"Tooch," Drew called to the younger runner at the back of the pack. He hoped Tooch would score a few regular season points and possibly qualify for the more important state meet at the end of the season. "This season you will score some points for us, lower your personal record, and.. ."

Tooch raised his arms over his head, sprinted to the front of the pack and shouted, "and bring home the gold!"

The guys laughed. "For which country?" joked Casey.

"For the River Hawks," answered Tooch.

"We're not a country," said Gil. "And we don't win gold medals."

"Whatever," said Tooch dismissively. He wasn't going to let facts slow down his fantasy. "You guys will be basking in my glory!"

"Basking?" questioned Casey. "Nice vocabulary!" It was a subtle joke aimed at Tooch's English. "Besides," he continued with the ribbing, "You can't be in the spotlight when you are hiding in Drew's shadow."

"Ouch!" laughed Gil. The joke was funny because it was true. Tooch shadowed Drew's every move, on the track, in the locker room, and even in the school hallways. The younger runner turned red with embarrassment.

Drew felt sympathy for Tooch. Maybe the joke hit a little too close to home and hurt his friend's feelings. "Don't worry, Tooch," he said, trying to smooth over the situation. "You'll have your moment someday."

The fire station in the Beech Hill neighborhood was the run's turn around point. During the XC season they would have continued on for another mile or so before heading back to school, but today they came to a stop in front of the brick building. Each guy took a turn ringing the historic fire bell that decorated the station's front lawn, a tradition River Hawk runners had been doing long before Drew's freshman year.

The easy pace kept the guys close together for the run back to school, and the conversation returned to the normal topics: school rumors, TV, music, annoying siblings, and anything else that could come up. The important topic for Drew had been settled, the distance guys were committed to run on the indoor team. Next he would have to secure the return of last year's best shot put thrower and starting left tackle of the River Hawks football team, Theo Marshall.

At 6'-7," 220 pounds Theo was a mountain of a man. Like most other football players, Theo couldn't run for more than a few yards with any speed, but he had a quick burst of strength that could launch the twelve pound shot far into the air. Theo was a five-pointer, and Drew had to have him on the team.

Theo always stood straight, making the most of his height. Since he often walked past others in the school hallways without stopping to look down or talk to them, kids thought he was aloof, but Theo was just serious. He didn't make small talk or spread gossip, and he never hazed the freshman. Theo was focused on his future.

In the center of the school hallway, Drew saw Theo's head and shoulders above the other students. His large frame moved forward at a steady pace knowing that the smaller kids would part way before him. Drew headed to Theo's locker to start his recruitment pitch.

"Hey, Theo," Drew greeted Theo at his locker.

"Little Man!" said Theo happily, breaking from his serious demeanor. It was easy for him to call people "little" from up there. "Congratulations on top ten. How'd you get your skinny ass to run so fast?"

"Thanks," said Drew. Although they had been on the same outdoor team last spring, the two guys had never spoken to each other before. Distance runners and throwers operated on different practice schedules and didn't sit close on the team bus. But the athletes of Aiken High had always silently kept an eye on each other, measuring who had athletic talent and deserved respect. Those that didn't measure up were left with their indifference. Having Theo, a football player, come out and acknowledge Drew's race was a big complement. "It was painful. My legs are still sore."

"Pain? Please..." Theo dismissed with a smile. "You play forty-four minutes of down lineman in a football game—offense and defense—and then you know what pain is." He pulled off his sweat top revealing his football practice t-shirt. His large bicep flexed as he pointed to the logo on his chest. "Playing football, that's what real River Hawks do."

"Yeah, well..." Drew changed the topic. "You are going to join the indoor team, right? We need you on the team."

"Team? Indoor is not a team sport. Football is a team sport. Basketball is a team sport. Track is just a bunch of skinny geeks running around." Theo was having fun teasing Drew. Switching back to his usual serious demeanor he gave his real answer to the question, "But, yeah. Coach wants me lifting weights and staying in shape over the winter, so I'll be throwing shot."

With that, Theo turned his attention to his locker, fished out the correct notebook, closed the door and without another word, turned to walk to class.

"One more thing," Drew said, trying to keep the conversation going. "You got to make sure the Loganikos brothers throw too." Mark and Michael Loganikos played defensive ends on the football team, but were not nearly as tall as Theo. Even though Mark was older than Michael by eleven months, they were both juniors. Last spring they had thrown shot on the outdoor team, and showed promise. Getting them on the team could add a point or three.

"You want me to ask them?" asked Theo. "Why don't you ask them?"

"Because they need to lift weights and stay in shape for football too, right?" Drew reasoned. "And they will do what you tell them. People listen to you, Theo."

"Of course they will do what I tell them," Theo joked, "because I will smash their Greek heads together if they don't." He was always reminding people of his size, strength, and toughness. It was a big part of his identity. His smile faded as he asked, "What's in it for me?"

Drew had anticipated the question long before this hallway meeting and had his offer ready. "You will be a co-captain. We've never had a field event guy be captain of the track team. You got ripped-off not being selected captain of the football team." Drew saw Theo wince at the reminder. It hurt Theo's pride that the tallest, biggest, and toughest senior on the football team had not been elected to be captain by his teammates, and Drew sensed it. "You'll be co-captain of the 1993 state champion Aiken River Hawks track and field team."

"Ha! State champions?" laughed Theo. "Get out."

"We have plenty of talented athletes in this school," Drew countered. "We get enough of them on the indoor team, and who is going to beat us?"

Theo was skeptical, but didn't have time to argue with Drew. "Okay, runner man." The switch from "little man" to "runner man" let Drew know that Theo was on board. "But," Theo asked, "what makes you think you can choose who's captain? You can't do that."

Throughout his life, people had been telling Drew that things were too difficult to do. It cost too much, so-in-so would never agree, or there was a rule against that. Some people seemed to give up before they even tried. Being a runner had shown him that difficult goals were achievable. Money could be raised, people could be persuaded, rules could be bent. With enough planning, training, and grit, Drew knew he could do things that others didn't think possible.

The bell rang, signaling students to leave the hallway and get into their next class. Theo turned to enter his classroom. Drew called out, "I can, and I will. Just get the Loganikos to throw, captain."

| 3 |

For two weeks the recruiting continued with Drew trying to persuade every available athletic guy at Aiken High to join indoor. Some he knew well from his classes, others he only knew by first name or just a nickname. Anyone with a decent athletic reputation was on his list. He had a little success. Two soccer players interested in the middle distance sprints, like the 300 or 600 yard races, agreed to run. Peter Constantine, the tall defenseman for the spring lacrosse team, was up for the hurdles. A few younger guys from the cross country team added depth, and hopefully some points.

Not everyone Drew asked wanted to run, and there was plenty of rejection. To some, running that much was too much effort. They wanted to rest for the winter season. Others just didn't see running as a sport. "I run in order to play a game," said the baseball team's third baseman. "I'm not going to run just to run!"

Then there were those who didn't think track was a team sport. "If I play on a team, I want it to actually be a team," argued another guy. "A team is where you all do the same thing together. Track is where guys do different things at different times. What's the point?"

Even the guys who did join were partially apathetic. Running indoor was something to pass the time between the fall sports and the spring season. They could take it or leave it, and if it weren't for Drew's positive enthusiasm, they would probably have left it.

To one and all, Drew's idea of a state championship was laughably unthinkable. There had never been a championship track team at Aiken, and none of them could envision how it could all come together. They could see each other's talent, but not how strong their collective strength could be. The lack of vision led to a lack of motivation: why invest all their energy and effort in an ultimately unattainable goal? They were willing to show up and get some exercise, but no one was buying the idea of a championship team.

The inspiration of a championship team came to Drew from another Aiken High team, the girl's indoor team. While they had never been state champions, the girl's team was a juggernaut, winning league championships year after year. Their coach, Ms. DeLuca, had the team organized and motivated. Girls from the cross country, soccer, field hockey and softball teams showed up every winter and ran, threw, and jumped their way to victory.

They were led by the McKinnon sisters, senior twins, Shelley and Linda, and their younger sister who's name Drew could never remember. The McKinnon girls were tall, beautiful, and fast—Drew estimated that together, including the high jump and relay, they were worth at least twenty points.

Shelley and Linda were more than talented athletes. They each belonged to several student clubs, wrote for the school newspaper, and one of them (maybe Shelley) was in the high school orchestra. Fashionable, put together, and always in a conversation, they had an air of confidence that made them, to Drew, intimidating. He had often thought of asking either Shelley or Linda on a date, but every time he approached them his mind shut down, his tongue stopped working, and he had nothing to say, let alone the ability to ask them on a date.

The girls team's best sprinter, Monique, on the other hand was a friend and confidant of Drew's. They had been friends for years since suffering through religious education classes together at their neighborhood church. The two had often provoked the ire of Sister Mary Burnadette for asking pointed questions about the Catholic doctrine delivered in class, and as a result had spent time together in detention. Ever since, their shared need to question the status quo, diagnose bureaucracies, and get to the bottom of things had kept them close.

When it came to keeping track of who was dating whom, or any other news in the hallways, Monique had the facts and could deliver them in a cool, dispassionate report. She fancied herself being an outsider observing the social drama of her classmates from a safe distance. To Monique, Drew's crush on Shelley and Linda was obvious and pathetic, and she often told him so. "If you're so in love with the Double Twins, just ask one of them out," she would tease. So it was no surprise that it was Monique who dropped the biggest bomb on Drew's state championship plan.

"State championship? The boys team?" she incredulously asked Drew as they walked the halls between classes. "How can a team win a championship when they don't even have a coach?"

Drew's eyebrows went up. "What's up with Mr. Morrissey? I just saw him two weeks ago for cross country," he said.

"Didn't you ever hear of retirement? He was old," said Monique.

Mr. Morrissey had been teaching and coaching at Aiken High for years. Drew's older brother and sister had him when they were at Aiken High in the early 80's, and even back then they joked about how old he was. Apparently early in his career, as a recent Harvard graduate, he had been a brilliant and motivated teacher who organized extracurricular activities and chaperoned field trips. But by the time the older Declan kids had him, almost thirty-five years into his teaching career, it was obvious Mr. Morrissey was just coasting.

In the first few weeks of the school year Mr. Morrissey would silently size up the students in his American history classes and decide what grade level they deserved, and that's the grade they got on every test, book report, class project or final exam no matter how the student performed. In fact, it was widely known that Mr. Morrissey did not read any of the papers students wrote. A few brave kids would write an opening paragraph about the topic assigned, say the Kansas—Missouri Border Wars of the 1850s, then write three pages about their favorite MTV VJ, followed by a single concluding paragraph on-topic, and get a B+. Drew knew one kid who, for a three-page paper, wrote out one page of material, copied it, copied it a second time, stapled the three identical papers together, handed it in and was awarded his predetermined C+.

Mr. Morrissey's coaching philosophy was similarly anchored by his worn-down fatalism. Fast kids ran fast, and the slow ones ran slow. Not once had the development of an individual runner been considered, and year after year, the track workouts he assigned never varied. The first 200, 400, 600 ladder workout assigned in December would be repeated each week until the last Tuesday of February.

That Mr. Morrissey finally retired wasn't completely shocking, but the news blindsided Drew. "Are you sure?" he asked.

Miffed that he questioned the integrity of her information, Monique answered with an emphatic, "Yes." Then she added, "I know because some other teachers had a retirement party for him at the Polish American Club. My mother does catering there."

Drew's mind raced with the information. At first he got sidetracked wondering why Monique's mother, who was Haitian, would be working in a Polish American Club. But then this type of thing was fairly common in Aiken as the immigrant families of the last century moved out into the suburbs, and new immigrant families from the Caribbean, Asia, South America and everywhere else moved in. People from all over worked and lived side by side.

Next Drew felt insulted and hurt that Mr. Morrissey didn't personally tell him about his retirement. He had been running for Mr. Morrissey for years and should have been told. But then, Drew had to admit, Mr. Morrissey had not been forthcoming with any of the runners or students that crossed his path over the years. There was apparently no exception for the best high school miler the school had seen in a generation.

Finally Drew concentrated on the most important issue. "If Mr. Morrissey isn't coaching, who is?" Drew asked. "They have to have a coach for us, right?"

It was Monique's turn to raise her eyebrow, and in mock deadpan she said, "Well now, they didn't really talk about that at the Polish American Club, now did they, captain Drew?" Before Drew could respond she added, "That's up to you to find out."

Neither Gil, Casey, or Tooch had heard the news about Mr. Morrissey's retirement. They were just as shocked when Drew told them, although Tooch, who hadn't known Mr. Morrissey as long, was not as upset. Running easily on a five miler through the streets of Aiken in the twilight of an early December evening, they considered the team without a coach. The first official practice for indoor was just a few days away, and the uncertainty was unbearable.

"What if they just have Ms. DeLuca coach the girls and boys teams," offered Gil. "They would save money by paying one coach for two teams."

"She can't go into the boys locker room," said Casey. "There's got to be a rule against that, right?"

"She knows track, that's for sure," said Drew. "Guys, I went to the athletic director's office but they wouldn't tell me anything. The secretary just said," Drew switched his voice to mimic the older woman, "'We do not disclose personnel issues.'" It was a lame impression, but Tooch laughed anyway. The other guys didn't bother to acknowledge it and continued the conversation.

"They have the Title Nine rule to make the girls teams better," Casey complained. "What about our team?"

"Yeah," Tooch added. "Us guys need Title Ten."

Laughing, Drew said, "No, it doesn't work like that."

Gil turned the conversation back to the point. "They have to give boys indoor a coach. You can't show up at a meet without a coach."

"Someone has to know who our coach is," reiterated Casey.

"I asked," said Drew, a little louder with the frustration of repeating himself, "and they wouldn't tell me. What am I going to do?"

The four runners ran in their small pack for a few quiet strides without talking. The rout they were running traveled along Aiken's most notable geographic feature, The Nantuc River. It was possible to run along the Nantuc for another ten miles through neighboring cities to the Atlantic Ocean, but they turned to cross one of the rusting steel truss bridges and headed back toward school. Running single file on the bridge's narrow metal sidewalk their footfalls clanged with each stride. On the far side of the river the four regrouped in a tighter formation close enough to talk.

"What about The Deuce?" Gil offered. "He knows about everything in the high school."

"Well, only if you want to know about football," Casey said.

"He's been working here forever," countered Gil.

Drew liked the idea. "Can't hurt to ask him."

"Wait—what?" interrupted Tooch, who was clearly not completely following the conversation. In an alarmed and shocked voice he asked, "Ms. DeLuca is coming into the boys locker room?"

"No!" shouted Gil, Casey and Drew, laughing at Tooch's confusion, and giving him a light shove.

"That's what you said!" Tooch defended himself.

The laughter continued down the sidewalk as the boys cruised easily back to Aiken High.

| 5 |

Mr. Stanley Martin was Aiken High School's athletic facility and equipment coordinator, but just about all of the kids used his nickname, The Deuce. The Deuce handed out uniforms, ordered all the buses for team trips, measured the chlorine in the pool, and made sure all the fields were correctly lined with chalk. His middle-age potbelly and slovenly clothes disguised that at one time he had been a fairly decent athlete. Fifteen years ago, when he was a defensive end for the Aiken High football team, he blocked an extra point kick, recovered the ball, and ran ninety-four yards down field, only to be tackled a yard short of the endzone. Had he scored the touchback, the River Hawks would have won the game and been crowned state champions. The two points he never scored haunted his Aiken High sports legacy, and left him with the nickname, The Deuce.

After graduating from high school he landed a job as the Aiken High School equipment manager, and had remained in that position since. It was an easy job, maybe too easy, for The Deuce was bored. Dealing with the school administration annoyed him and made him perpetually grumpy. The job he really wanted was head football coach, but even though he had

29

been involved with the team for years, and at one point had been the special teams coach, he had always been passed over for the top position.

Underneath his tired and irritable demeanor was a guy who loved sports, the Aiken High River Hawks, and especially now that his own children were nearly high school age, the kids that played the games.

Most afternoons after classes had ended The Deuce could be found reading novels inside the equipment room surrounded by years worth of gear, memorabilia, and clutter. When Drew Declan walked into the equipment room interrupting the quiet part of his day, The Deuce's annoyance was palpable.

"You got a hall pass?" The Deuce asked before Drew could say a word.

"You don't need a hall pass after school," Drew said.

"I didn't ask you what time of day it was," The Deuce said sharply. "I asked you if you had a hall pass."

"No," said Drew, controlling his annoyance. This was such a typical football coach thing to do: accuse the younger person of some imagined infraction just so they can feel like the top dog. That was one of the reasons Drew stopped playing team sports. All these "ra-ra," tough-guy coaches just bugged him. Threats of punishment from an overbearing coach didn't motivate runners. It was the inner desire to improve, compete and succeed that motivated runners like Drew.

"Well, you need a hall pass next time," continued The Deuce. "What do you want?"

"Do you know who the boys indoor coach is going to be? I asked in the AD's office but they wouldn't tell me," said Drew.

"Ha," chuckled The Deuce. "No. They won't tell you," he said thinking of his own battles with the AD's office. Then his mood lightened and he added, "But don't worry, they got a new guy coming in who's going to be all right."

Gil had been right, Drew thought, The Deuce did know. It seemed that Gil always came up with the right answer.

"He's a young guy. First coaching job. Just got married." The Deuce blurted in short sentences, as if he were delivering a scouting report on an opposing football player. "Was the 5,000 meter Ivy League champion. Went to Pittsburgh, I think."

Drew winced. The University of Pittsburgh wasn't in the Ivy League. So either the new coach wasn't a 5,000 meter champion, or he didn't go to Pittsburgh. The Deuce probably got the school wrong, Drew thought.

"He's got a degree in biophysics. He's an athlete. He knows his stuff," concluded The Deuce.

Drew took in all the information, and was relieved. For days he had worried, but in hindsight it had been silly to think that the school would not give them a coach. The indoor team was important to him, and anything that could possibly go wrong, or ruin his plans was something he worried about. Knowing for sure that they had a coach, and that they would be allowed to show up at meets, was a load off his mind.

There was only one thing that The Deuce had left out. "What's his name?" asked Drew.

Grabbing a sheet of paper from one of the piles on his desk, The Deuce squinted and held the paper a few feet from his face until the type came into focus. "Ethan Pilette. Must be a French name," remarked The Deuce.

Listening to The Deuce was always an exercise in sifting the useful information from the useless. Whether Coach Pilette's ancestors were French or not was, to Drew, useless. That he was a distance runner, a champion, a first-time coach, and, apparently, a biophysicist, were useful.

There were still many unknowns for Drew as he left The Deuce's office and walked home from school. Would this new, young coach know how to coach the sprinters and shot putters? Could he get the team into top shape? Would he be the right coach to galvanize the team, help them score enough points, and bring home what Drew desired the most, a state championship?

He'd get some answers the next day after school, when boys indoor had its first practice of the season.

| 6 |

The old Aiken High School, built in the Collegiate Gothic Revival style so common of public buildings of the Depression Era, was constructed of red bricks formed and fired in a brickyard merely two miles away. The town elders showed their civic pride by splurging on the state's most renowned architect, and were rewarded with a building that won praise for its elegance and functionality.

In the late 1960s the Baby Boom generation had overcrowded the old school, and the citizens of Aiken voted to raise their taxes for a needed addition. This time the priority was maximum size for minimum price, and the Aiken Civic and Educational Construction Oversight Committee produced an oversized structure that dwarfed the old building. Constructed almost entirely of poured concrete, the addition had none of the charm or elegance of the original structure. By 1993, years of exposure to the elements had turned the addition's light colored exterior into a dismal gray. The new building towered over the original, appearing like a muddy avalanche rolling over the old brick school. In the bleak months of a Massachusetts winter, the addition was reminiscent of the bland and lifeless buildings normally found in the Soviet Union.

The two buildings, connected with short bridges and tunnels that allowed students to move from class to class, maintained their own heating systems. Despite its newer and more efficient forced hot air, the addition's classrooms and hallways were generally a good ten degrees colder than the old, radiator-heated school. For students, stopping on a bridge to add or remove a sweat top between periods was as routine as finding the right lunch table in the cafeteria.

The money saved by not paying for an aesthetic design or an effective heating system left funds available for construction of an indoor pool and an athletic field house. The field house, which everyone referred to as "The Nest" was a "multi-use facility." The rubberized floor of The Nest was covered with dozens of overlapping colored lines that marked the courts of different sports. Yellow lines for the four tennis courts, powder blue for indoor soccer, green for three basketball courts, orange for volleyball, cyan for badminton, and black for wiffle ball.

The most important line was the red one. Encircling all other lines in a perfect oval, the red line hugged the walls the length of the building and curved sharply near each end. This one simple line was the Aiken River Hawks' home track, where the team held their practices and home meets. Drew had run lap upon lap over the last three years, training, racing, and winning. He was as familiar with it as any other surface in the world. The rubberized floor matting still had some springiness that made Drew feel faster than when he ran on the roads or even on the outdoor track. He had put in so much time and effort running there, so many memories had been made training and racing, that it had become something more important than a simple red line to him. It was his track. Much like how football players felt they were defending their football field's grass turf from opponents, Drew believed, on his home track, in The Nest, no other runner could beat him. No other team could beat his River Hawks.

There was one more home field advantage to The Nest's' red line. The track was 200 yards long. Not 200 meters or 220 yards, which would have been one-eighth of a mile. Due to the slipshod construction The Nest was built too narrow, and a regulation size track did not fit. The red line was 200 yards long. To race a mile the runners would turn eight times around the track and still have about three-quarters of a lap to go.

Even though the distances were clearly marked and the officials warned the runners at the start of each race, Drew was always amazed how many opponents would unleash their final kick too early, only to find an additional three-quarters lap to go after the eighth lap. Drew and the other River Hawk milers knew they could outlast their opponents by holding back a little energy on the eighth lap, and pressing hard for the final three-quarters lap.

It was in The Nest, in the center of the red line's oval where the River Hawks gathered to meet their new coach. About three dozen of them milled around, waiting for the first practice of the season to start. Mixed and matched in different colored t-shirts and shorts they certainly didn't look like a team, and could have easily been mistaken for any other club or group in the school. Despite the eclectic attire there were subtle similarities. They wore running shoes, not the basketball sneakers most wore in the hallways during the school day. They were thin, athletic, and bursting with energy.

The team was impatient to start their workouts. The indoor teams, both boys and girls, had first use of The Nest after school. At the end of their allotted time the basketball teams would take over the courts and kick out any remaining runners. But mostly, they just wanted to do something.

In the middle of the group Drew heard his teammates' discontent.

"Are you sure we got a coach?" questioned Gil.

"He's probably just running late," joked Casey. "Get it? Running—late!"

"Is today's the right day, right?" asked Tooch with a worried tone of voice.

Drew decided it was up to him to get the practice started, and spoke up. "Hey, guys. We have to get our warmups in. Gil, take the distance guys and start over there," he instructed, pointing to the far curve of the track. "Middle distance guys, we're going to start over here on the straight away."

As the boys started to separate into different groups Drew approached a muscularly built African American kid. "Stats," Drew greeted him. "Good to see you." Donell Timlin, the River Hawks' starting running back, had racked up the most yards-per-carry and receiving yards in school history. His explosive speed and athleticism made him one of the best athletes in Aiken High, and he loved to recite his football statistics to anyone who would listen.

Stats didn't reply, he just nodded his head in acknowledgment. He had a serious face and his eyes bore an intensity that made people think he was either angry or ready to start a fight. He was a tough kid from a tough part of the city, and he used that toughness on the football field.

Drew knew instinctively that he couldn't order around Stats, or any of the sprinters for that matter, so he changed his approach. "Hey, do you think you could get the other sprinter guys going on a light warm up?" he asked easily. "Two—three laps would loosen up the hamstrings."

"If that coach doesn't show," said Stats while slapping his hands together then flying one arm out to his side, "I'm, like splat." With a definitive look on his face he added, "You know what I'm saying?"

Stats was an excellent sprinter—a five-pointer, for sure—and Drew didn't want him to walk out before the first practice was under way. The other sprinters seemed to follow Stats's lead, and if he trained and raced hard they probably would too. If Stats left the team, scoring any points in the sprints would be hard.

"I heard he's just running a little late," Drew said with a confident nonchalance. "By the time you guys get warmed up..."

A blast of a whistle interrupted all conversation, and everyone turned to look at the short, impossibly thin man with the whistle. Coach Ethan Pilette walked into the center of the track expecting everyone to circle around him. They didn't. Everyone had stopped talking and running at the whistle blow, but they just watched, frozen in place. The whistle blew two more times, the sound bouncing off the cement walls of The Nest.

A whistle, thought Drew incredulously. Football coaches use whistles. Basketball coaches use whistles. But track coaches never use whistles. They just yell.

Coach Pilette let the whistle drop out of his mouth and dangle on the rope around his neck. He grabbed his clipboard, shuffled a few papers, and finally looked up to realize that no one had gathered around. Surprised at his loneliness in the middle of The Nest, he awkwardly fumbled for the whistle and gave a much feebler blow.

Deciding to rescue the new coach from this embarrassing lack of cooperation, Drew walked over to the coach and called out, "All right, let's bring in here!" At his words the thirty teenagers moved over and formed a ring around Coach Pilette.

Without making eye contact and his shaky hands fumbling with the papers on the clipboard, Coach Pilette gave a short speech filled with the most common and tired clichés in athletics. Phrases like: "There is no I in team"; "When one of us wins, we all win"; and "What you will get out of this season, is what you put into it."

The team half-heartedly listened. Teenagers are expert lecture-listeners. They hear lectures from teachers, coaches, priests, and parents, and are quick to decide whether they can tune in, or out. Like sizing up a substitute teacher to see if they will have to do any actual schoolwork in that period, the team heard the wavering voice of Coach Pilette and instinctively knew they had nothing to fear.

Peter Constantine, the lanky lacrosse player, decided to have some fun. "Hey coach," he broke in. "When can we bring out the high jump mats?" Coach Pilette was startled by the interruption, and a few of the guys started to laugh as Constantine added, "Some of us need to take a nap."

Anger flushed through Drew. This wasn't football where the coaches demanded a "yes, sir," "no, sir," type of interaction, but interrupting any coach in the middle of his talk? Constantine had always been a goofball, but this was just too disrespectful. Drew opened his mouth to yell at Constantine when he heard a loud voice behind him break in.

"Shut the hell up, Constantinople!" yelled Theo Marshall, purposely confabulating Constantine's name as a measure of intimidation. "You gotta listen to the coach." Theo's words silenced the runners. All side conversations stopped and everyone was paying attention. "On this team," continued Theo in a measured and emphatic voice, "we listen to what the coach has to say." The Loganikos brothers who flanked Theo nodded their heads.

Drew realized that Theo was taking his captain position seriously. It could have been so easy for him to laugh along with the other guys at this skinny and insecure new coach, but he hadn't. Theo was making a statement. He had bought into the idea that this was his team, and he was speaking out to keep things under control.

"Yeah, that's right." confirmed Drew. There was a murmur of approval in the crowd. Drew turned back to Coach Pilette who had been watching the scene more as a spectator than the leader of the team and said, "What's next, coach?"

Coach Pilette finished his prepared remarks then talked about the actual workouts he expected the team to do. The coach's tone was more comfortable as he presented the technical information. He spoke of warmups, complex dynamic stretches, plyometric exercises, human biology and interval training.

The change in Coach Pilette's demeanor got the team interested in what he was saying. This coach was describing athletic training in a professional and scientific way, and was using terms they had never heard of. Their old coach, Mr. Morrissey, had been old school, and the training had been simple. They had run the same workouts week in and week out. This new coach was offering a new, more scientifically based training system that promised to bring out the best in each runner, not just the gifted ones.

The team broke up into four groups: throwers, sprinters, middle distance and long distance. Drew, being a miler, would alternate days training with the middle distance guys and the long distance guys. For this first practice he would run on the track with the distance guys: Casey, Gil, Tooch, and the others.

"What are capillaries, again?" asked Casey as they started to jog into their first 400 yard interval. Coach Pilette had thrown out a lot of new terminology.

"Capillaries?" laughed Tooch. "Don't they turn into butterflies?"

"Small veins," answered Gil as they started picking up speed. For this first workout coach had scheduled them for 4 x 400 with a 200 rest. "They bring blood cells to your muscles."

Coach Pilette had given Drew a clipboard that listed the workout and the times he expected each runner to hit for their intervals. The new coach had done his homework. He knew the names and abilities of the runners on the team and had goals for each runner.

Theo ordered the Loganikos brothers and some younger throwers to carry out and set up the shot ring and block in the center of the infield. While they worked on that he lugged out his brand new, giant boombox. About ten inches tall and two feet wide, it was powered by six size D batteries, and could throw enough decibels to fill up the field and grandstands of the outdoor track. When he loaded his latest CD and pressed play the opening riff of "Pump Up The Jam" rattled off the walls and ceiling of The Nest.

"Ready. . . and..." said Drew as his group approached the start line. "Go!" The runners took off, settling into a pace that would take them to their interval time.

Soon there was a weave of runners around the red line. The boys and girls teams seamlessly alternated their intervals to make the most efficient use of the lanes. On their rest laps runners jogged in the outside lanes clearing the inside for runners who were up to speed. Coaches were shouting out split times, and occasionally someone would shout out some encouragement to another group. Drew was in his element, running around the track, passing and being passed by his teammates and friends. After all the long distance runs of XC, it was pure fun to lean into the corners of the track and test his speed. Dopamine flowed in his brain, and he felt light, powerful, and fast. It was the first workout of his last season of indoor, and he wanted to soak up and enjoy every yard.

After jogging through his cool down mile Drew decided to check in on the sprinters. In one end of the infield he joined Stats and the others in their post workout stretch.

"How did he know?" asked Stats abruptly. Drew interpreted the question to be, "How did the new coach, who had never seen any of them run or play before, come up with a detailed athletic plan for each runner?"

"Research," answered Drew. "He must have looked up our times from last spring's outdoor track. Maybe he looked up your football stats, Stats."

Stats smiled. "That's dope," he said approvingly. "He was researching me? You think he knows I had the third most YAC in the state?"

It took Drew a moment before he got it. Yards After Catch was a football statistic that Stats was proud of. "Yeah, I bet he knows," said Drew.

"Funny, he looks all squirrelly, eyes wide, like he is about to get run over by a truck, or something," said Stats, giving his appraisal of the new coach. "But, if he has the knowledge, if he has the stats on all thirty-eight players, if he has Stats's stats," he said, referring to himself in the third person, "then I'm in on that. All in. You know what I'm saying?" It was apparent that Coach Pilette may be nervous and awkward, but he obviously knew his stuff.

Drew held in his excitement. If Stats was "all in" on the coach and the team, then he could count on his points in the meets. The other sprinters that took Stats's lead would also train and perform. He nodded his head and held up this open hand to Stats. "We are going to win this year," he said, solidly.

As Stats reached out to return the high-five, Drew was never more confident about anything in his life. They were going to win.

| **7** |

Luckily for the River Hawks, their first meet of the season, which came with only ten days of training, was at Chester High. Like Aiken, the town of Chester sat on the Nantuc River and had once been a prosperous mill town. In the years following World War II, the big manufacturing companies left the northeast United States for less expensive employees in southern states or even overseas, and Chester's economy had been particularly hard hit. Fewer jobs led to fewer people and the city's population had diminished. The number of students at Chester High was a fraction of what it had once been, and their indoor team just didn't have enough runners to be competitive.

The River Hawks easily won the meet. Stats, Drew, and Constantine easily won their races. Gil and Casey went one-two in the two mile. Theo and the Loganikos brothers swept the shot put. The most surprising result came from Tooch. He ran well in the mile, recorded a PR and finished third, earning his first varsity point for the River Hawks.

The girls' team also cruised to an easy win over Chester, as was expected. Monique moved up from her usual 50 yard dash to the 300 yard run, easily won, and later led off the winning 4 x 440 relay team. The McKinnon sisters, Shelley and Linda, and their younger sister, dominated as usual.

So both teams were in a good mood when they boarded the two buses back to Aiken. On the way to meets the boys generally went in one bus and the girls in the other, but on the way home, especially when both teams won, the buses filled up co-ed.

Drew waited around before boarding, keeping an eye on which bus the McKinnon sisters went on. That would be his bus too. He bet that Shelley and Linda would sit in the same seat and he wanted to get a seat near them. He didn't know them as well as he wanted to despite being on the same team as them for a few years. The only missing part of his plan was a topic of conversation. What would he say to them? He could congratulate them on running a good race, or talk about their baton hand off in the relay. No, that would be awkward, and embarrassing. He always seemed to be awkward and embarrassing around Shelley and Linda.

As he climbed the stairs to the bus and turned the corner to look down the aisle, he saw what he had hoped for. Shelley and Linda sat together in a seat about halfway down the bus, and right in front of them was an open seat. Joy and anguish hit him at once. Joy, in that he was right about them sitting together and an open seat nearby. Anguish that he had to go through with his plan and start a conversation with the two girls who were chatting casually with each other, oblivious to his presence.

Walking down the aisle of the bus his heart began beating faster and harder than when he cruised through his two races in the meet. Why was his heart out of control, pumping furiously when he had the cardiovascular fitness of a top athlete, he wondered? Why could he talk to football players, soccer players, lacrosse players and convince them to run track, and yet he couldn't start a conversation with two girls he shared the same sport with? Why could he pass tests, confidently make persuasive arguments to teachers, coaches, and officials, but as he walked closer to Shelley and Linda, his mind was frighteningly blank?

There was a tap on his shoulder and a man's voice broke through the fog in Drew's head. "Hey, easy run today, Drew," said Coach Pilette. Coach was sitting by himself in the first bench of the bus. Drew realized that he hadn't actually taken any steps down the aisle and had just been standing at the top step for the last few moments.

"Ah, thanks," stammered Drew, now starting to take a step forward.

"Yeah, hey..." Coach continued in his unsteady way. Then, pointing to the open seat next to him, he added, "Have a seat."

The options raced through Drew's head. He could keep on walking, as if he had never heard the coach's invite. He didn't want to miss this perfect chance to sit next to the McKinnons. On the other hand, it was hard to refuse an invitation from a coach, and it would be disrespectful to ignore him. Drew already had several conversations with the coach this season and each of them had been awkward in their own way. When Drew suggested that he, Theo Marshall, and Stats be tri-captains for the team, he had lengthy arguments prepared to convince the new coach of the wisdom of his idea. But Coach Pillette just blinked a few times and nodded approval. Now Drew wondered what weirdness would come up in this conversation. With a little annoyance, and a good measure of relief of not having to approach the McKinnons, he sat down.

"A 4:42 is not near your PR," Coach Pilette began, analyzing Drew's time in the mile that day. That was true, he had run a much faster mile time last year. Obviously Coach had done his homework and knew Drew's times from the spring. "It's actually a disappointing time for how much base you built up during the cross country season."

Any angst or worry Drew had over the McKinnons was gone. His attention was now squarely focused on this implied criticism from his new coach. Was Coach expecting him to run a PR when there was no real competition in the race? Getting a bit defensive Drew replied, "Well, I did win the race."

"So what?" countered Coach Pilette. "There was no one in that race near your speed. You just cruised through it." Shaking his head he added, "Looked like you were going to stop for a beer along the way."

Was that a joke, Drew wondered? He hadn't seen a glimmer of humor from the coach yet. And it was, technically, inappropriate for a coach—a representative of the school administration —to joke about drinking to an underage high school student. The school hallways were littered with anti-drug and drinking posters, and all the teachers and guidance counselors preached that message ad nauseam. There were hundreds of kids at Aiken High and Drew knew there were many who were involved in that world. By his senior year he had piloted his life away from those kids, and had little contact with them. The kids he knew best, those on the sports teams or in his college-bound classes, weren't involved in the drug and drinking scene, and Drew had little awareness, or interest in it. He knew kids from his grade school and middle school who had taken a different path, and in Drew's estimation, those kids were wasted talent. They were smart kids who were barely making it through school, or great athletes who couldn't make a team if they tried. He had always been someone who could see the talents and abilities in others and knew if they could harness that skill, anything could be possible. To see kids squander their talent was tragic. As Gil once said on one of their runs, "They call it 'dope' for a reason."

He pushed all these thoughts aside, deciding to keep the conversation about track. "Scoring points is good. We have to score to win the meets," he said.

Coach Pilette nodded in agreement. "But for a runner with your ability, 'good' isn't good enough. I have big goals for you this season, and for you to run a sub 4:20 mile you have to take every race of the season seriously."

Drew's eyebrows shot up. "A sub 4:20 mile?" he said, his voice rising. That was much faster than he thought he could run. A 4:20 mile would score a lot of points and possibly make him a contender in the state meet. He didn't think it was possible. There were always one or two guys out there running sub 4:15. "Our real goal for the season should be a state championship for the River Hawks," said Drew.

Now it was Coach Pilette's turn to be surprised. Despite all of his research on the individual runners on the team, he had obviously never considered the team as a whole. As if to tamper Drew's expectations, Coach started to explain, "It takes a really deep team to win a championship. We have some good runners..." He left the unfinished sentence hang, implying that the

River Hawks didn't have the athletes to get the necessary points. Then Pilette tilted his head as a new thought came to him, and in a brighter tone of voice he said, "but I do have a new runner joining the team next week who could help."

If Drew had been surprised by the sub 4:20 mile prediction Coach Pilette had just made, it was a pleasant surprise. Like a window opening to a previously unseen opportunity. But the phrase, "new runner joining the team" was a shock. It was Drew who had recruited the team's best runners. He had sweet-talked, promised, and cajoled every decent athlete in the school who wasn't currently on another winter season team. He had even passed out photocopies of the registration forms and made sure the guys had their parents sign and return them. He was the one who watched the varsity basketball team tryouts, figuring out who wasn't going to make it, then recruited Asher Dane to be their high jumper.

Who, an incredulous Drew wanted to know, was this guy from the University of Pennsylvania (which was in the Ivy League—not the University of Pittsburgh as The Deuce had said) to tell him who was going to join his team?

And where was this "new runner" coming from? Drew felt that he knew every single worthwhile athlete in the school, even those guys who did non-school sports like karate and fencing. None of them were just going to show up and start running track without him knowing about it.

Maybe the "new runner" was an inner-city cousin of someone already at Aiken High. Occasionally a kid would show up at school claiming to be a resident of Aiken but really lived in a tough section of Boston. Their family decided that it was best for the kid to live with an aunt, away from a violent neighborhood and gangs of the city. Kind of like the kids from Central America, Cambodia, Haiti, and elsewhere, they had left their home for a better chance in Aiken. Drew knew that Stats's cousin, Keith, used to live with him. It often took a while for these kids to fit in. Some never did.

"Did he just move here?" Drew asked skeptically. "Like, from California or something?" It was the last possibility he could think of, that some family got transferred to the East Coast. Even that was unlikely since so many manufacturing jobs had left the city.

"No. I don't think so," answered Coach Pilette earnestly. "I had a meeting with Roberta Drain. She runs the PRISM program. Do you know about the PRISM program?"

Oh, Drew knew, and he didn't like where this was going.

There were actually two high schools in Aiken. Aiken Memorial High School, home of the River Hawks, where about 2,100 kids from all across Aiken went to school, and the PRISM school that housed the fifty-odd students who had been expelled from Aiken High. The city was required to provide an education for all students, so they created this second school for the most troubled and disruptive kids. The majority of PRISM kids were caught selling drugs—probably marijuana—on school grounds. Some kids had been expelled for getting into too many fights. Drew had heard a rumor that one kid had been expelled for bringing a pistol to school.

The new emotion that took over Drew was fear. He believed the rumors about fights and guns. Without ever knowing or meeting a PRISM school kid, he believed the stereotype of what a PRISM kid must be like. Someone so bad and so violent that they just didn't get suspended from Aiken High, they got expelled—for good.

"Well, Mrs. Drain has a student that is going to be integrated back into the regular..." Coach Pilette realized he had used the wrong word and tried to correct himself. "Ah, he's going to be mainstreamed... No... assimilated?" Neither seemed to accurately describe the situation. Coach looked up at the ceiling and scratched his chin searching for the appropriate word.

Drew's mind raced ahead, attempting to decode what Coach was trying to get across. "Integrated" was often used to describe a racial situation. Like in the 1970s when the Boston schools were integrated and they bused black kids to neighborhoods that were predominantly white, and white kids to neighborhoods that were mostly black. But Aiken High was already integrated with kids who were white, black, Spanish, Asian, you name it—all in the same school.

"Mainstreamed" was code for kids who had a developmental disability. There were a handful of kids like this who took some or all of their classes at Aiken High. Joey Banes, the team manager for the football, basketball, and baseball teams was a full time student. JB, as everyone called him, had one of these disabilities—actually Drew had no idea what kind, but it didn't matter. JB was a great kid, loved sports, and was a fixture on the three big teams.

"Assimilated" didn't really have any meaning for Drew, and it seemed, neither for Coach Pilette. He was still silently searching for the correct word.

"Who is it?" broke in Drew.

"His name is Jeremy Lamonda," answered Pilette. "Mrs. Drain says he's looking to get back to being with other students. This could be really good for him." With a positive and comforting smile he added, "We could help him out."

Drew didn't know the name. First, he made a mental note to ask Monique if she knew anything about this kid. Monique knew everything about everyone in town. Second, what did Coach mean by, "We can help him out?" Who did he mean by "we"? Was Coach asking for his help? What was he expected to do for this new kid?

"Can he run?" Drew wanted to know. "What is he, a sprinter? Distance? How many points can he score?"

"We'll find out," said Pilette, turning forward to look out the front window of the bus. "Mrs. Drain wants us to let him fit in." And with that, Coach Pilette fell silent. The conversation was over and Drew was left sitting next to the coach at the front of the bus. He looked over his shoulder, and sure enough, the seat in front of the McKinnon's was now occupied. Constantine, the goofball, was there chatting away with the sisters.

In past years Drew could easily gauge how the team was shaping up after the first meet: who the strong runners were, or what the team was lacking. It had always been so straightforward and logical. But this year, with a new coach, and so many unproven runners on the team, the future seemed chaotic. Keeping them all focused on the ultimate goal, the championship, with so many distractions and outside interference was going to be harder than he thought.

Normally after an easy win the bus ride home to Aiken would be fun. On this ride, with so much uncertainty about the team, and being stuck next to the untalkative coach, it was one of the longest rides he could remember.

| 8 |

Workouts on the day following a meet were often light ones. Even though Coach Pilette's clipboard had a down-to-the-minute schedule of stretches, warmups, exercises, and intervals for each group, the day's run would be easy. Drew and Tooch were able to join Casey and Gil, and some other distance runners for a long run outside.

With most sports teams—and really any youth activity—practices were organized, scheduled, supervised and overseen by coaches, teachers, parents, or some combination of all three. The adults were there to instruct, correct or reprimand as they saw fit for the duration of the practice. Less and less often, it seemed, were kids given the time and space to organize and play sports among themselves. By their teen years they were tired of the restrictions and wanted to break free of adult nagging.

Distance running was the sole undertaking where kids could be on their own. No one ever supervised the long runs. For cross country practices, Mr. Morrissey would announce the distance the team was to run that afternoon, then leave for the day. Drew never knew a coach, or any adult for that matter, who could keep up with the team on a five mile run. Coach Pilette, who just finished his college career could have, but he was busy with the sprinters, jumpers and throwers. It was the guys on the team who decided which route to take, policed that everyone ran the whole workout, and ensured they all made it back to school. Not only were the runners unsupervised, they were unaccounted for. The coach did not even know where in Aiken his runners may be because the runners themselves didn't decide their route until after they left The Nest.

On long runs there were no overbearing coaches, no teachers threatening detention, no parents with impossible expectations. They were untouchable. They could relax and have fun with their sport. They ran free.

Running on the roads of Aiken, they were easily identifiable as the high school running team. They were bunched together in two or three tight groups, and ran at a constant, steady pace. Any other random group of teenagers would certainly be walking, not running the smooth, mile-after-mile gait of real runners. Occasionally one of the other Aiken High coaches punished his team by forcing them to run distance on the roads, but they stood out because they wore the same practice uniform. Distance runners never wore the same clothes.

With December temperatures in the low 30s, the distance members of the River Hawks indoor team wore a mismatch of multicolored sweatshirts, windbreakers, pants, hats and gloves. Gil had lost his gloves and was wearing a second pair of socks (he said they were clean) on his hands as mittens. Moving down the sidewalk of the city center they looked like mannequins that had just busted out from a secondhand clothing store.

"So you're saying you didn't have time to look for your gloves," said Casey who was grilling Gil about the socks. "But you had time to get a second pair of socks?"

"They're clean, I tell you," pleaded Gil. "And mittens work better than gloves anyways."

"But they aren't mittens," countered Tooch. "They don't even match."

"Will you get athlete's foot on your hands from those?" laughed Casey.

Luckily for Gil, at this point, about two miles into the run, they had dropped weaker distance runners who had fallen off the pace. They were running in a tight pack of four, and no one but his friends could hear the ribbing he was taking. No embarrassing details would get back to school.

Gil's discomfort reminded Drew of his socially awkward bus ride home with the coach.

"Hey, have you guys noticed Coach Pilette being even more awkward than usual lately?" he asked the group. "I mean, he's always kinda awkward, but recently even more?"

Glad that the subject of conversation had changed, Gil said, "He's not awkward when he's talking about running."

"Just the rest of the time," added Casey.

"No, I mean like, at the end of practice the other day he gave me the clipboard with the next day's workout. He told me to get everyone started because he was going to be late," complained Drew.

"So?" questioned Gil with a shrug. That didn't seem to be noteworthy.

"I thought you liked that," added Casey. "Telling people what to do. Giving orders. You know, acting like this is all important." He was on a roll with his jokes.

Drew thought he had started a conversation about the coach but it somehow wound up being about him. Even though Casey was joking, it felt like a bit of an accusation. True, he did often tell people what to do, but only because he, in most situations, could look ahead and realize what needed to be done. So he was just getting people to do what they obviously should be doing.

"I don't order people," he replied, stressing "ordered" as if it were a horribly offensive word. "Just sometimes you have to move people to get stuff done," he offered lamely.

"Get what done?" asked Tooch.

"I don't know. Stuff," stammered Drew. Trying to find an example he offered, "Like, getting all the guys to join the team. Would everyone be here, running every day at practice, if you didn't make them want to?"

"I'd be running no matter what," said Gil, defiantly.

"What do you mean, make them want to?" Casey wanted to know.

The runners had finished running through the commercial section of Aiken and turned to complete the loop back to school. Storefronts became fewer and the city blocks were mostly filled with two and three family homes. The final incline from downtown to school was not steep, but it had a constant 2 percent grade that would cause the weaker runners to fall even further behind.

The four runners cruised along comfortably, their easy breathing allowing them to talk. Any kind of topic could come up on a run, even ones that would never in a million years be discussed in the hallways or lunchrooms of school. Sure, they would talk about silly stuff, but late in runs, when the dopamine was flowing the topics could be deep and meaningful.

"Sometimes people can't see a good idea until you show them," began Drew. "When they see it, they want it. So you show them what you want," he said, building up to a big finish, "and then they want what you wanted them to want."

"That's so true!" yelled Tooch.

"What crap," said Casey dismissively.

"Like I said," said Gil, getting back to his earlier point. "I was going to run if you asked me or not."

That was true, thought Drew. Gil and Casey were real runners who had a passion for the sport that kept them going mile after mile. Their success in running had translated into other parts of their lives and made them more confident and stronger people. Gil was at the top of his class academically and was striving just as hard to be the valedictorian his senior year. For Casey the confidence and camaraderie earned from running bolstered him against the fractured and unhappy family life he faced at home. Drew had heard their stories over so many long runs together. Unlike the rest of the athletes on the indoor team, to Drew these guys were worth more than the point value they could score for his team. They were members of his pack who shared the same love for his sport. "That's 'cause you're smart and you get it," concluded Drew.

"What?" laughed Casey. "Unlike young Tooch here?"

"Hey! I get it too," complained Tooch. He reacted to the joke by balling a fist and whacking Casey on the shoulder. Casey tried to dodge the hit and wound up knocking Gil off stride. While trying to maintain his balance, Gil's foot clipped the back of Drew's shoe making him stumble forward. After about half a block of stumbling, pushing, and laughing, the pack settled back into their normal pace.

They ran around the front of the old school building to the back of The Nest. The guys stopped in the parking lot and stretched while they waited for the slower runners to finish up. After a final head count to make sure they all made it back and no one had been hit by a car, they turned to head in.

Just a few feet from the door was a short yellow school bus with its motor idling. A light cloud of exhaust plumed out of its tail pipe filling the air with carbon monoxide. Dusk had fallen and the streetlights above cast a shadow between the bus and the building. The runners, now all accounted for and a bit rested, filed between the bus and building.

With a loud bang the heavy aluminum fire door flung open from within, spreading a path of light on the ground between The Nest and the bus. Whoever had kicked the door open was standing with his back to the runners, one arm up in a wave, his second arm down in front of his waist. It looked as if, Casey would later say, the kid was taking a piss on the track's outside lane.

"More of this, tomorrow!" the kid yelled to no one in particular. He quickly jerked his arms back, spun around toward the bus, then froze when he saw the runners.

The sound of the door being kicked open and the bright light from inside had stopped the guys in their tracks. None of them knew who this kid was or what he was doing on their track.

They stood still, on the edge of the lighted path between the building and bus, like reporters at a press conference watching a celebrity walk by.

Jeremy Lamonda was the first to recover and said with a scowl, "What are you looking at?" He was tall and his muscles were well developed. Definitely not a distance runner, thought Drew. Maybe not a runner at all. With his quick moves and jerky action he had the presence of a wrestler. . . or a fighter.

With two quick steps Jeremy was almost at the door of the bus while he continued his rant. "You sacks look like you escaped from a refugee camp." Then he yelled, "Go back to Cuba. No one wants you here!" With that, he curled up his left bicep as if to show off his muscle, slapped it with his right hand, and hooted, "Waaat, waaat, waat!"

The instant he hopped on the bus, the door closed and the engine roared. Like a limousine fleeing from the paparazzi at a New York City nightclub, the bus, with its only passenger, sped off leaving the runners in the darkness outside The Nest.

The guys stood silently for a moment piecing together what they had just seen. No one had seen him before, but he had to be Jeremy, the new kid from PRISM. He must have just finished his first practice on the track while they were out on the roads. He seemed as volatile and violent as they had feared.

"So, you're saying," said Gil breaking the silence, "You lured him to be on our team?"

Drew knew he didn't have to answer. Gil didn't really believe he tried to get that kid on the team, but once again he felt defensive and wanted to set the record straight. "Sometimes," he said, "things are just beyond your control."

| 9 |

Lazer's tail could still wag as fast as a puppy's, but the rest of Lazer was slow and stiff. When Drew's family adopted the dog twelve years before they gave him the name because he could zip around the yard at light speed. Even through his middle years Lazer had great endurance, and Drew had often grabbed the leash and taken him on his runs. The first quarter mile or so was rather fitful with Lazer stopping to pee on every tree, rock and fence post, but after that warmup he either decided to keep up with Drew or had run out of urine.

Lazer was now beyond middle age—in his old age, actually, and could not keep up with Drew on any runs. A simple walk around the neighborhood now took forever, with Lazer slowly plodding along behind. Drew didn't even bother to put the leash on the dog anymore because, let's face it, Lazer wasn't going anywhere fast, and there was no risk he'd run away. Lazer just wanted to go along and stay close to his master, Drew.

It was obvious to the whole family that Drew was Lazer's favorite. Wherever Drew was in the house, whether at the dinner table, watching TV in the living room, or doing homework in his bedroom, Lazer was sure to be within a few feet, keeping an eye on him, waiting for any sign that they would be going on a run, or walk. Drew's parents would sometimes take the dog for a walk, but Lazer seemed to think of that as a second-tier adventure, showing his disappointment by half-heartedly wagging his tail in low, incomplete sweeps.

Greg and Jen Declan, who were eleven and nine years older than Drew, had moved out on their own long ago, so almost out of necessity, Lazer attached himself to the one who was still around and most fun to play with.

Like many evenings Drew came home from practice to find that Lazer was the only one home to greet him. The dog, who had been asleep in the living room, rolled off the couch and trotted into the kitchen, tail wagging full strength.

After Jen moved into her college dorm, Drew's mom got a job selling real estate in Aiken. It was a job with flexible hours and, in the first years, she was always home in the afternoon when he got back from school. With her success, the part-time job had slowly turned into a full time career. So many of her friends who had kids the same age as Greg and Jen were now empty nesters. They had decided to sell their homes in Aiken and move to nicer places in the suburbs or along the seacoast, and their realtor of choice was Ellen Declan. With the hectic schedule of real estate closings and open houses, his mom could be home after school for three days in a row, then not home for the next ten. Drew could never keep her schedule straight.

His dad had a much more predictable work schedule, but that didn't translate into him being around more. This being a Wednesday meant that his dad wouldn't be home either. A couple of years ago Rich Declan received a nice promotion and now worked three days a week in New York City. Every Tuesday morning, before Drew got up for school, he left for the airport, then returned home very late Thursday night. Neither parent had been available to attend any of Drew's races this season. The mid-week meets just didn't align with their schedule, they said.

Just as he tossed his backpack onto the kitchen table and before he could even open the fridge, the phone rang. Drew was surprised to find his brother Greg on the line.

"Mom's not home," he said, not waiting for Greg to ask.

"Yeah, I know," replied Greg. Launching into his intended topic he said, "You'll never guess who I ran into today."

True, thought Drew. He would never guess because he didn't care to guess. Whenever his brother and sister came home to visit their parents the conversation always turned to something Drew found completely boring. Health insurance, mortgage applications, mutual funds, tax deductions, wedding plans —how many hours of wedding-plan discussion had he endured before Greg's wedding? Any subject that someone in their late twenties may ask their parents for advice was something that an eighteen-year-old high school senior couldn't care less about.

Drew's eyes glazed over with boredom and he managed to mumble out, "No, I don't..."

"Your coach," interrupted Greg. He was always interrupting Drew, as if his thoughts were more important. "Ethan Piller!"

"You mean Ethan Pilette?" Drew corrected as a little interest crept back into his voice.

"Yeah, Pilette," replied Greg. "I didn't make the connection at first. Julia was talking to his wife."

"Where did you guys meet him?" asked Drew. Greg and his wife Julia lived in a nearby town and Drew wondered if Coach lived in the same town too.

"At the hospital. At a baby birthing class," said Greg. He and Julia were expecting in a few months. If anything superseded wedding planning conversations on the boredom scale it was definitely baby conversations. His mom was planning on having a baby shower for Julia at their house soon, and Drew was planning on going for a very, very long run during that time.

"Coach Pilette teaches birthing classes?" Drew asked with skepticism. He knew he had a degree in physiotherapy, but did that make him qualified for this?

"No!" yelled his brother, laughing. "His wife is pregnant too. The four of us are taking the class together."

"Oh," said Drew, embarrassed at what was, in hindsight, a dumb question.

"Yeah," continued Greg. "They are due in a few months, too."

Drew had no reply. After getting momentarily interested that his brother knew his track coach, Drew settled back into a more comfortable, disinterested mode. Whether his coach was having a baby or not didn't really make much difference to him.

Sensing Drew's lack of interest Greg added, "This is big stuff —having babies. You'll find out. It's important."

"Yeah," Drew reluctantly acknowledged.

"He says you're a big help to him," said Greg. "Practically running the team, he said."

"We do have a pretty good team," said Drew, glad that the conversation was turning to running. "We have good sprinters and throwers from the football team, and there's this kid who got cut from the basketball team who's actually a good high jumper. I think we can win it all this year."

"Yeah, well..." Now it was Greg's turn to lose interest. "That's all I got for now. Tell mom to call me when she gets in," said Greg, ending the phone call.

Lazer climbed the steps to the second floor behind Drew, and followed him into the bedroom. After circling a few times over the soft part of the rug he laid down, took a deep breath, and let out a sigh. He would patiently watch Drew do his homework, looking for any sign that they might go for a walk.

The posters on the bedroom walls could have been a display at the Running Hall of Fame, if there were such a thing. Right over the bed was Rod Dixon, eyes shut, hands in the air celebrating his New York City Marathon win, while the second place finisher, Geoff Smith, lay on the ground, a few feet past the finish line exhausted and dispirited in defeat. Over the bureau was Eamonn Coghlan, the Irish miler leaning into a banked curve of an indoor track. Bill Rodgers, in his hand-drawn Greater Boston Track Club t-shirt, hung on the closet door. Smaller pictures cut out from magazines had running greats like Joan Samuelson, Alberto Salazar and, of course, Steve Prefontaine. Right next to the bedside lamp, in her University of Wisconsin singlet, was the blond, blue-eyed, NCAA champion Suzy Favor.

Flopping down his notebook on the desk Drew pushed aside an unruly pile of newspaper stories that told of his cross country success. They weren't front page stories—those were reserved for the football and soccer teams—but ones from inside the Aiken Chronicle sports section. Usually the coach or one of the parents wrote and submitted the stories, never a reporter.

Occasionally a picture would accompany the story, but only when Aiken was running against a nearby town that was also in the paper's distribution area.

It occurred to Drew that all of his clippings, trophies, ribbons, even all of the pictures of him running, were here in his bedroom. There wasn't a picture of him taken in the last three years in the rest of the house.

Lazer had just let his eyes droop closed when Drew jumped up and headed back to the stairwell. Excited and thinking that there might be a walk in his future, the dog lumbered after him. But Drew had stopped on the stairs looking at the framed family pictures running down the wall.

Graduation photos of Greg and Jen from both high school and college. Jen's graduation from med school. Mom's Realtor of the Year award. Greg and Julia's wedding. For all these important family milestones Drew had just been a spectator, stuffed at the edge of the group shots.

At the bottom step Drew came to the one solo picture of him. Shaggy-haired and before he had his braces, he was pictured in his little league baseball uniform, resting an aluminum bat over his shoulder. Taking the picture off the wall he wondered how long ago this picture had been taken.

Why was this the picture his parents thought should go on the wall of family accomplishments? He wasn't a baseball player anymore. He hadn't been, well, since this picture was taken. And he hadn't been a good baseball player either. This wasn't him! "I don't even like baseball," he said out loud to the dog. Baseball, with all the pitching changes, throws to first, gum chewing and spitting, was the most boring sport ever invented. Imagine actually having time to chew gum while playing a game.

Deciding that they weren't going for a walk, Lazer circled around and laid down at the foot of the steps, letting out a long groan of disappointment in the process.

It wasn't like his family didn't like him or care about him, he thought, looking up at the pictures of graduations, promotions, and weddings, it was just that he hadn't done anything important yet. Anything he did or could do had already been done by his brother and sister. Nothing he could do was "wall worthy."

He sat down on the floor next to Lazer who thumped his tail vigorously on the floor. What did Casey say to him today? "Acting like this is all important," he had said. Was it important? Was high school track really that important? Shaking his head he conceded that, compared to life's big events, it was not. Heck, half of the kids on his own team would probably rather be playing something else.

Yet, that word, important, wouldn't leave his mind. It felt important to him. Running and winning was exciting and challenging—and fun. He looked forward to the races, the workouts, and the long runs with the guys. It was something that he was really good at. It filled him up with confidence and pride.

Back when he was nine years old, just after his last season of little league, Drew was thrown into his first race: a 10K road race. Greg and Jen were both home for summer vacation and had decided to run Aiken's Fourth of July "mini-marathon." Dragging their little brother along for the run was a normal part of the family dynamic, so Drew found himself in a crowd of three hundred adults at the starting line.

The first three miles saw the field stretch out to a long single file line with Drew and his sister jogging together near the back of the pack. Neither Jen nor Drew had ever run this far, and they were starting to learn that keeping the pace, especially in the summer temperatures, was exhausting and painful. Just past four miles Jen fell behind. The heat radiating off the asphalt had taken its toll on the out of shape joggers, and one by one, runners in front of Drew wilted. He was as hot and tired as any of them, but the thrill of passing adults made him press on.

Drew had been passed over when the city's Babe Ruth baseball team was selected. His hand-eye coordination, which was average at best, made him a liability on any basketball team. He was too skinny to play Pop Warner football, and his ankles were so wobbly on ice skates that his parents refused to sign him up for hockey. But here he was, passing adults. He was good at something.

The cramp in his lower abdomen grew tighter, and the rest of his body desperately wanted to stop and rest, but he found that he could push through the pain and keep running. *Don't listen to the pain,* he thought, *just keep going.* Every person he passed was one more person that he was better than.

With just a block or two to the finish Drew recognized the shape of the runner in front of him as his older brother Greg. Rather than running upright and smoothly as he normally did, Greg's stride was a little wobbly and his head tilted to one side. Drew saw his opportunity. He was so hot and dehydrated that he was feeling cold chills run down his neck and torso, but he was now focused on passing the brother that had dominated every aspect of his sporting life.

Cranking up his leg turnover to a sprint, he felt his legs, which moments before were heavy and sluggish, turn numb. The road seemed to pass under his body without his sneakers landing. It was as if his body ended at his waist and he was riding on someone else's legs and feet. The sensation of not being in control of his own body was startling, but it didn't stop him from closing the gap.

Drew dashed by his unsuspecting brother yards before the finish line, and for the first time in his life became the best Declan at something. Whatever else Greg and Jen could do— drive cars, go to college, become a doctor, work at important jobs, or anything else—Drew would always know that he was a better runner than them.

From that day on Drew was a runner. Not a jogger or just a fitness buff—a runner. He would train to be fast and win. In every race he would push himself to pass as many others as possible and to succeed. Running was who Drew Declan was. It was the center of his character, his faith, his passion, and he loved it. And when you love something, it is important.

"That's right," he said aloud to Lazer. "It is important!" Lazer started thumping his tail on the floor sensing the adrenaline radiating from Drew.

If you love something and it is important, thought Drew, then it is ok to be passionate about it, work hard at it, and give it everything you have. He loved running and nothing was going to stop him from winning.

"You want to go for a walk?" asked Drew. The word "walk" had the desired effect. Lazer climbed to his feet, and tail wagging, followed his master to the door.

The track team locker room was the only one that didn't change teams throughout the school year. While the football locker room became the basketball locker room in winter, and then the baseball locker room in spring, the track locker room maintained a nice consistency through the cross country, indoor and outdoor seasons. Being located in the basement of the new part of Aiken High, not the original brick building, it was also relatively new and clean.

The downside to the locker room was its lack of a hot shower. The heating system of the modern building was weak, barely able to keep the upstairs classrooms at a warm temperature in winter, and its water heater was never designed to heat enough hot water to shower an entire team. So for a warm shower the guys had to walk through the tunnel to the basement of the old building where the shower room was old and dingy, but had hot water.

As a freshman, Drew had refused to take a shower after practice because he was uncomfortable walking down a corridor in co-ed school wearing nothing but a towel. First off, it was just embarrassing to be almost naked at school. Second, there was the fear, not unfounded, that someone would sneak up behind him and pull off his towel, leaving him completely naked in front of everyone in the hallway, including the girls team.

The older guys on the team had to lay down the law, and let everyone know that if they ever tried to pull off someone's towel, there would be retaliation. Since the fear of mob violence was greater than the fear of embarrassment, most guys, while still cautious, walked to the showers and back in their towels without incident.

In their first locker room meeting of the season Drew reminded the team of the long standing hallway-towel rule. To emphasize the point further, Theo stood up and in a serious and menacing voice proclaimed that if he heard of any "towel-grabbing crap" he would be first in line to "pound the living snot out" of the offender. Later, Casey said that he was going to point out to Theo that snot wasn't actually "living," but was too afraid to do so.

It was in the locker room before practice where most of the guys met for the first time of the day. Tooch, who was a sophomore and had classes in a different part of the school than the upperclassmen, was usually the first one in the locker room. "Captain Declan is in The Nest!" he greeted Drew with a big smile. "What are we going to run today?"

The only thing that superseded Tooch's pride and enthusiasm for being on the team was his devotion to the team's leader, Drew. At the end of every running season, when some athletes moved their gear to the baseball or lacrosse locker rooms, Tooch would find a newly abandoned locker and move a little closer to Drew's. This season the team's captain and his number one supporter had lockers side by side.

Coming from Cambodia when he was school-aged made the transition to urban America very hard, and Tooch struggled to fit in and make friends. He had been self-conscious of his poor English skills, and often kept silent when outside of his family. Being small for his age, he had never been good at the school-yard games played at his elementary and middle schools.

When Tooch joined cross country his freshman year, he was a shy and silent kid who was anxious about being an outsider in a locker room of older guys who all knew each other. On the team's first training runs, he quietly hung on to the back of the pack, worried that if he got dropped he would get lost and not find his way back to the school.

Things changed ten days into the season when the captains led the team out on the Gut Run. The long, punishing run was a tradition of Aiken XC to see which of the new runners were there because their parents wanted them to participate in an after school activity, and those who really wanted to be a River Hawks runner. If a kid could stick with the lead pack through the summer heat, hills, and fast pace, it was proof that he belonged. The ones that fell off pace wilted in the heat and seldom showed up at another practice again. No one got cut from XC, but they could definitely be left behind.

Tooch, overheated and in obvious pain, struggled to hold onto the pack in the last mile, but finished the Gut Run within a few minutes of the leaders. As the runners cooled down in the shade of the building, one of the older guys on the team walked over, handed him a water bottle, and asked his name.

Tooch had to say his name a few times before the older runner could get the pronunciation right, but once he got it, he complimented the freshman by name. "Tooch, that was a gutsy run," said Drew Declan. Reaching out for a handshake he added, "Welcome to the team." Just like that, Tooch knew that no matter what he may have been before the Gut Run, from that moment on he was a River Hawk runner.

Now in his fifth season of running, he was more confident in his ability to keep up with the guys, both in running and in the verbal combat that takes place among teammates. Being part of a team—an important part that scored points—was great for his self identity and confidence. When Tooch walked the halls between classes he always wore his River Hawks XC running jacket.

"We're on the track today, Tooch," answered Drew tossing his gym bag down at the foot of their lockers. Drew had chosen his locker because it was closest to the door and he could keep track of who showed up for practice. "I bet Coach Pilette is up-stairs with a couple of clipboards right now."

"Does he even know where our locker room is?" Tooch wondered. Unlike the girls' coach, Mrs. DeLuca, who spent time before and after practices checking in on her team, Coach Pilette remained by himself on the track waiting for the boys to inter-act with him. The only other adult who occasionally ventured into the boys locker room was The Deuce. If some football player kept his River Hawks football practice jersey, which was technically school property, The Deuce would take the jersey right off the kid's back and return it to the equipment closet for next year.

As the rest of the team entered the locker room to get ready, Drew would greet them. Stats entered the locker room with one of his fellow sprinters, Keith, and approached Drew. Keith had been one of the guys that joined the team with Stats and had been a surprise addition to the team. He had moved up from the 50 yard to the 300 yard race, and showed that he could score some points. Both sprinters carried themselves with a tough serious demeanor, but while Stats could loosen up and joke around, Keith always remained aloof and dismissive of anyone not in his tight circle of friends.

"Hey, Dec," Stats greeted Drew. He stood with his shoulders back, standing tall, less than a foot from Drew. "Number 39 is no good. He's a bad dude. You know what I'm saying?"

Even with his aggressive stance and sharp tone of voice Drew knew he didn't have to fear the sprinter. Stats always saved his aggressiveness and fury for the playing field and track, and never wound up in an actual fight. They had talked enough over the years and had mutual respect for their athletic talent.

Still, it took a moment to decode what Stats was saying. "He's a bad dude" must be a reference to Jeremy, the new guy on the team. "Number 39?" There were about that many guys on the team. Was Stats actually keeping track of the number of runners on the team, Drew wondered? "You mean Jeremy?" asked Drew. "Are there really thirty-nine guys on the team?"

"Yeah, and yeah," replied Stats, answering both questions. Then picking up on the first train of thought, said, "He's bad. Like they dredged him up from the old times." Pointing over his shoulder at his fellow sprinter he added, "Keef says he disrespects the brothers all the time."

Keef? Drew was almost sure the kid's name was Keith. Was it a nickname Stats had for him, or had Drew been calling him the wrong name? More importantly, what was clear was the phrase "disrespects the brothers." Stats was one step short of saying this new kid, Jeremy, was racist. That was a serious charge to make in a school with kids from so many different ethnic backgrounds. Having someone like that around was sure to drive kids off the team.

Looking at Keith to get confirmation, Drew asked, "Do you know him well?"

Shrugging his shoulders with disinterest Keith mumbled, "Just business."

For two guys who grew up together and called each other cousin, Keith and Stats were very different people. Behind his tough-guy exterior Stats was observant and alert. If asked a question he always gave a thoughtful answer. Keith, on the other hand, didn't seem to have much curiosity about anything that didn't concern Keith. It was amazing that Stats had enough influence on Keith to get him to join the team and run well.

Drew was about to ask what kind of "business" Keith was talking about when they were interrupted by a man's voice. "Donell. Keith. Where are your practice jerseys?" demanded The Deuce using Stat's first name. "You were supposed to turn them in at the end of the season," he said, referring to the football season.

Stats stepped forward to defend himself as Keith slipped back into the crowded locker room. "Hey, it's all I have to run in with my River Hawks colors. You know what I'm saying?" said Stats.

"You have to return the football jerseys," repeated The Deuce a little exasperated. "You can just run in your track stuff."

"But there isn't any River Hawks track stuff," countered Stats waving his hand around the room at the patchwork of non-matching shirts and shorts. Then straightening up he added, "I need my red and black colors. I have to show my River Hawk pride when I work out. You know what I'm saying?"

The Deuce's resolve wavered. He loved the Aiken River Hawks and never wanted to dampen the enthusiasm of an athlete that shared his River Hawks pride. "Well, turn them in at the end of the season," he relented. "I want them back before baseball, and in good condition so I can hand them out next season," he said pointing a finger. "I mean it this time."

Stats said with a big smile, "Promise, promise."

Drew was impressed with Stats's maneuvering. He played to The Deuce's weakness and got him off his back until spring, by which time The Deuce would have long forgotten about the football practice shirts. Maybe now, he thought, was the perfect time to up the ante.

"You know what would be great for our team," he said, stepping forward to The Deuce. "New uniforms. We don't have matching uniforms."

It was true. Most of the distance guys had kept their River Hawks Cross Country singlets and still raced in them. Some guys wore black tank tops with a red River Hawks logo. Drew and some others wore the outdoor uniforms, red with white and black lettering. The high jumper, Asher, wore a white t-shirt from the Aiken High drama club. The different uniforms didn't affect the team at track meets since each competitor got a number to pin onto their shirt. It was the number that got recorded and scored for the team.

"So?" replied The Deuce with a shrug.

"So, we are a team," said Drew, making his argument. "We should look like a team."

"Oh, that would be cool," interjected Tooch who was following the conversation from behind Drew. "And jackets! We should all have those new jackets!"

The Deuce gave a small chuckle at the enthusiasm. Shaking his head, he said, "Not going to happen. Your budget was used up buying the new high jump mat that kid sleeps on all afternoon," pointing a finger at Asher.

Asher, his mouth agape at the accusation, ran his fingers through his floppy blond hair and replied with deep earnestness, "Not sleeping. Meditating. I think we would all benefit from increased mindfulness."

A groan went up from the other guys in the locker room. Constantine playfully threw a balled-up t-shirt at Asher, missing his head by an inch or two and hitting his locker with a thud.

"Yeah, I'll put your new yoga pants in next year's budget," said The Deuce to a round of laughs. Then switching to his commanding tone of voice he bellowed, "You guys get upstairs. You got a practice to get to." Quickly turning, he exited the room as suddenly as he had entered it.

Drew realized that he had lost any chance of getting new gear from The Deuce. What started as a promising opening when Stats played to his sympathies was slammed closed with Tooch and Asher's interruptions. If he ever had the chance again, Drew thought, he would make sure to close the deal.

| 11 |

When the first female runner crossed the 1980 Boston Marathon finish line in near record time people in the running community were suspicious. There were reports that she may have jumped into the race with a few miles to go. Other runners in the race who had run a similar time did not remember seeing her on most of the course. Her legs, they noticed, weren't as muscular as the other elite women who trained by running ninety miles or more a week. In her post-race interview she was asked about her interval training leading up to the race. She replied that she didn't know what intervals were, and actually asked the reporter for a definition.

All serious runners, including the real 1980 Boston Marathon winner, Jacqueline Gareau, know what interval training is. High speed running for a certain distance with intervals of rest in between to let the heart rate recover. It is the essence of every track workout.

Coach Pilette, in his first season coaching young runners, was brilliant at devising interval workouts that maximized the runners ability, and at the same time kept the training interesting. No two workouts were identical. He may not have been the most personable coach, but he made up for it with his commanding knowledge of the sport. The River Hawks were training at a level that old Coach Morrissey had never considered possible.

This day, Coach Pillette scheduled a ladder for the middle distance and distance guys—220, rest—440, rest—660, rest—880, and they would repeat the ladder three times. A tough workout like this often turned into a mini competition among the different runners. The faster sprint guys like Constantine and Keith would have the advantage in the shorter intervals, while Casey and Gil could be the leaders in the longer distances. Drew felt that, as a miler who needed both speed and strength he should be at the top of all the intervals.

As they were running their warmup laps the side door to The Nest slammed opened and Jeremy Lamonda strode in already wearing his running shorts and t-shirt. It didn't take long for him to cause a disruption. Walking past the girls team as they stretched he ogled them and said just loud enough that only they could hear, "Which one of you wants my babies?"

The girls scowled at him in anger. Monique spoke back sharply, "Shut up, fool."

The angry reaction seemed to make him happy. He laughed, grabbed his crotch and taunted, "It's right here. You know you want it!"

The nasty comment infuriated the whole team and a bunch of the girls yelled at him. "Get lost!" yelled one. The commotion caught the attention of Coach DeLuca, who walked over to see what was bothering her girls team. Jeremy, seeing an adult stepping into the situation, slunk over to where the boys team was finishing stretching.

Coach Pilette, buried in the pages of his clipboard, missed the entire incident. Normally the players on a team instinctively gravitate toward their coach and create a loose ring of athletes around him, but that was not the case with Coach Pilette. He was often, as was the case then, standing by himself in the middle of the infield. With the warmup and stretching parts of practice complete Drew decided to get things going and start the main workout.

"Coach, can I start lining everyone up?" he asked as he approached.

Quickly looking at his watch, Pilette replied, "Oh, yeah. It's time. Line them up." Looking up to meet Drew in the eye for the first time he added, "Make sure Jeremy is in your group. He is going to be running middle distance too."

Drew absorbed this new assignment without changing the expression on his face. He was going to hold in his. . . what was it? Disappointment? Dislike? Anger? Fear? He had to acknowledge to himself that it was fear that gripped him whenever he had to interact with Jeremy. In the two weeks Jeremy had been coming to practice, he had done at least one insulting, obnoxious thing each day. People avoided him as much as they could.

The guys on the team said that other PRISM students weren't like Jeremy. Most were unremarkable except that they had made some ridiculous mistakes and got tossed out of Aiken High. If given another chance they would fold into the rest of the student population without much notice. The rumor was that Jeremy's acerbic and insulting qualities made him disliked at PRISM too.

"Let's line it up, guys!" yelled Drew making his way to the start line on the oval. Casey, Gil, and Tooch started to get ready.

Constantine and a few others made their way over. Jeremy lingered by the folded grandstands talking with Keith.

"Let's go, guys," said Drew as he approached the two, interrupting their conversation. "We're starting now."

The boys stopped talking and turned to stare at Drew. Jeremy paused for a long, silent moment looking right at Drew, as if he were ready to bark out a challenge. Then without acknowledging him walked past Drew to the starting line.

"880?" complained Keith. "I not running an 880. Why do I need to run that far if I'm just racing the 300?"

Most football players complain about running anything over a 40 yard dash, so Drew wasn't surprised to hear the complaint. He adopted his usual positive approach and said, "The longer intervals will make you stronger in the last third of your race. It will make you a winner."

Keith scoffed out a dismissive laugh. Shaking his head he walked past Drew to line up.

Coach Pilette was on the inside of the oval with his stopwatch ready in his hand. "Ready, in two. . . one.. go."

The boys took off quickly with Constantine breaking to the front of the pack. Drew was late to the line and trailed near the back through the first turn. It was a quick pace, but not an all out sprint. They had a long workout ahead, and were just easing into it. Drew tried to move up in the pack but with only a little more than two laps in this interval it was hard to maneuver around his teammates.

As they approached the 220 mark Coach Pilette looked at the stopwatch and started yelling out, "28, 29, 30, 31. Good job."

Then he added in a most coach-like manner, "Don't walk! Jog the rest intervals!"

Gil jogged next to Drew. Looking around to make sure no one else could hear, and with a nod toward Jeremy and Keith asked, "What's up with those two? Are they friends?"

"I don't know," answered Drew. He was going to say more but this was the shortest rest interval and the team bunched up as they approached the start line. Drew didn't want to be caught in the back of the pack again so he scooted up a few spots as the coach counted them into the 440.

Again the pace was quick but smooth. Even though the team had done a mile warm up earlier in practice, their legs were really loosening up now. Constantine was in the lead again followed by a small group of guys that included Jeremy, who was running very well. Over the years Drew had seen many runners start out a race or workout too fast and wound up finishing weakly. He assumed this was going to happen to Jeremy now. Jeremy was an athletic kid, but there was no way he had the endurance to finish a long workout like this with any strength.

On the final straightaway of the interval Jeremy surged ahead, passed Constantine and took the lead. Coach Pillette counted them into the finish line, "65, 66, 67, 68, 69, 70. Good job. No walking."

Turning around and looking at Drew who had come in behind Constantine, Jeremy scoffed, "I thought you were supposed to be good."

"It's a long work out," replied Drew. In his mind the real workout, the part that made you a better runner, was the third set of the ladder. Anyone could run well early on, but the toughest runners could hold their speed when they had been working hard and were tired.

"That will give you plenty of time to look at my ass," said Jeremy to a smattering of laughs from the guys.

Drew winced at the insult, and he wished he could think of a good comeback, but his mind was blank. He was angry at Jeremy, but he was more hurt that the other guys laughed along against him.

The runners started to bunch up, getting ready for the beginning of the 660. Drew moved up to get a position at the lead of the group, but was cut off by Tooch who was also making his way to the front of the pack.

Jeremy, who towered over Tooch, extended his hand over to Tooch's head, and flicked his knuckle off the back of Tooch's ear. There was an audible "snap" of finger against skull, and Tooch yelled in shock. "Out of my way, munchkin," said Jeremy.

Tooch looked like he was about to react, but the size difference between him and Jeremy made him reconsider.

Anger flushed in Drew, and he was about to say something to the jerk, but Coach Pilette was counting them into the 660, "Two, one, go!"

Normally the longer intervals would be run at a slower pace, but, if anything, the lead pack was running faster. Constantine held the lead for the first lap, but Jeremy and Drew pulled ahead of him before they had run the first 220. Jeremy had the inside position making it harder for Drew to pass on the corners. Whenever Drew tried to pull ahead on the straight-aways, Jeremy would match the pace and slightly drift out into the second lane to block him.

Off the final turn Drew accelerated and both boys crossed the line at the same time, seconds ahead of everyone else. Neither one spoke in the rest interval, partly because they were out of breath, but really because they were now focused on finishing stronger than the other.

Through the 880 and into the mid-part of the second ladder Jeremy and Drew pushed the pace, never more than a half of stride apart. The other boys were finishing further and further behind. What had started as a mid-season training workout to improve the team's fitness had turned into a two-man, do-or-die grudge match for supremacy. Both guys were going to put all they had into beating the other.

Finally Coach Pilette realized something was going on. He jogged over to the runners during a rest interval. "You guys are well under the target times. Did you read the clipboard?" he asked. There was no answer from them. No eye contact. No acknowledgment. They were focused on regrouping for the final ladder. "I want you to back off your pace a bit," Coach added. "You don't want to burn your racing legs in a workout."

But Drew did want to burn. He wanted to use every bit of energy to beat Jeremy. Yet under his smoldering anger was a nagging doubt. How could this kid Jeremy show up without the heavy training and mileage of a cross country season and still hang with him through this work out. If Jeremy could run with him now, would he be the faster runner after a few weeks of training?

It may have taken Coach Pilette a while to realize that a battle between Jeremy and Drew was raging, but everyone else in The Nest had caught on much earlier. The girl's team kept an eye on them. The shot putters, Theo and the Loganikos brothers, moved over to the edge of the infield to shout encouragement to Drew as runners flew past. Asher, the high jumper stood up on his mat to get a better view.

In the 220 and 440 of the last ladder Jeremy and Drew turned it up more. Constantine could barely hang with them for a lap. Coach Pilette, his face turning red with embarrassment, realized he had lost control of the workout. Drew and Jeremy were hip to hip around the track. Each surge by one runner was matched by the other. Each stride was equal to the other's. Each fast split time was clocked the same.

The boys basketball team entered The Nest, getting ready for their practice. Normally they would start lazily shooting jumpers and layups as the track team was winding down their work out, but they had been alerted to the battle. JB, the team's manager, had run down to their locker room and spread the word. Now, they lined the outside of the far turn, hooting and hollering at the spectacle.

Down to the last interval, the 880, Drew and Jeremy were both tired and worn out. Drew knew he couldn't just tie Jeremy anymore. A tie to a kid that just walked onto the team—his team—and not just any kid but such a jerk like Jeremy, was as bad as losing. Drew knew he had to win, and win decisively. The whole team was watching. The girls team was watching. And with the basketball team along the curve, he knew this race would be talked about all week long in school.

The runners approached the starting line. The other teammates lined up along the straightaways as spectators. JB put his basketball at his feet, reached out with his hands and clapped.

Clap—clap—clap. It was a slow and rhythmic beat. The other basketball players laughed. They all loved that kid like their own little brother, so they put their balls down and joined JB. Clap—Clap—Clap.

"Ready, in three, two.." began Coach Pilette counting the runners into the start. Theo and the Loganikos brothers joined in. Clap! Clap! Clap!—faster and louder. Stats and the sprinters. Clap! Clap! Clap!—louder and stronger. The girls team. CLAP. CLAP. CLAP. The sound bounced off the walls and filled The Nest. Asher reached up to cover his ears.

"Go!" said Coach Pilette. Drew tore off and into the first turn, gaining the inside position. Jeremy hung right on his shoulder. The clapping had broken its rhythm and people just yelled and cheered as the boys flew by.

On the straightaway of the second lap Jeremy made a surge pulling slightly ahead of Drew's right shoulder. But Drew had matched the new pace as they hit the curve and was able to lean into the turn and regain a slight lead.

Now it was Drew's turn to press the pace. Out of the turn he accelerated into the tunnel of cheering kids on the straightaway. Kids were jumping up and down, waving River Hawks sweat tops in the air, shouting their heads off. JB jumped out onto the track within inches of the racers, shouting and cheering wildly. One of the basketball players protectively pulled him back so he wouldn't get run over.

Now on the last lap Drew dug down deep and poured on the pace. He swung his arms, drove his legs into the track, and pushed his body forward through the air, faster and stronger. He couldn't see Jeremy in his peripheral vision, so he knew he had a lead, but he didn't know by how much, or if Jeremy could make one last surge.

He rounded the last turn. The boys basketball team was jumping up and down, holding back JB. The infield swelled with cheering teammates. Drew flung his body forward and over the finish line. He stopped, put his hands on his hips and bent over to catch his breath. Looking up to see how far back Jeremy finished he was surprised to see that the second runner to finish was Tooch.

Across the other side of The Nest's infield, through the crowd of clapping teammates he saw Jeremy heading for the door. He had given up on the last lap and never finished. For a brief, unmistakable, moment they made eye contact. Seeing the anger in Jeremy's face Drew knew that this would not be the last battle between them.

Suddenly someone jumped on Drew's back. It was JB. "Captain Declan wins the race! Wins the race!" he shouted. A crowd of kids surrounded Drew with congratulations.

"JB, I thought you didn't like track?" joked Drew. "Maybe you want to be our trainer now?"

JB paused and thoughtfully said, "No. I'm the basketball trainer. I'll stick with basketball. Or football. Or baseball." People laughed, then started to mill away from Drew.

From across The Nest came the loud clang of a door slam. Through the door's window Drew could see the short school bus open its door for its only passenger, and within a moment the bus drove away from Aiken High.

| **12** |

The Aiken High River Hawks competed with seven other cities in the Northeast Massachusetts Athletic Conference (NEMAC). The teams raced each other throughout the regular season before heading to the more important state meet in late winter. Each week the NEMAC coaches sent each other the results of their meets, along with the times and points of each finisher. For the sport of indoor track, these coaches' race results were the closest thing to a scouting report, and Drew loved poring over them, sizing up the other teams and taking note of the best runners across the league.

At the first practice after the Christmas break Drew was surprised to see Stats looking at the coach's clipboard with the NEMAC results. "Anyone close to your time in the 50?" he asked as he, Gil, Casey and Tooch approached Stats.

"They're nothing," Stats replied dismissively. "I can beat them all."

That wasn't true, Drew knew. There were a few runners who had run times close to Stats's, and one guy had already had a faster time so far this season. "What about that kid from

Seacoast Regional?" asked Drew. "You have to beat him if we're going to win a championship."

"Seacoast? Man, I hate them," said Stats, shaking his head. Seacoast Regional had a large student population and had strong teams in every sport. Their football team had crushed the River Hawks this fall in a humiliating loss. "Besides," he added, "we aren't scoring enough points."

Drew was confused. "We aren't scoring enough points? How do you know?"

Stats looked up from the papers on the clipboard with a look on his face as if Drew just asked the dumbest question in the world. "I have the stats right here," he said shaking the clipboard. "In the first three meets they scored 162 and a half points —most in the league. We only scored 158. They're better." Then he frowned and demanded to know, "How did they score a half a point?"

"High jump," broke in Gil. "You can have a tie for third place in the high jump, and the teams split the point." The group of runners looked over to the high jump area where Asher Dane was lazily loafing on the soft foam mat. Two girls were sitting on the edge of the mat near him.

"Figures." said Casey disgustedly.

"Wait a minute," interrupted Drew. He had gone through the clipboard earlier and there were no team point totals. Over the last few seasons he had never seen team point totals on the coaches' results. "Where did you get the total points?"

"I just told you," said Stats shaking the clipboard in Drew's face. "I have the stats right here."

Gil tried to get clarification. "You added it up in your head?"

"Wow," said Tooch.

"Did you use a calculator?" asked Casey.

"Calculator? Who needs a calcul. . .?" Stats was getting defensive and a bit angry. "I left my calculator in Geology class," he mocked. "YES, I did it in my head! What makes you think I can't do math?" he accused.

"I couldn't add it up in my head that fast," said Tooch. The other guys heartily agreed and that seemed to mollify Stats's anger.

It dawned on Drew that Stats's nickname was Stats, not because he was always talking about his own athletic statistics, but because he could instantly calculate all the statistics in his head.

Drew brought the conversation back to track. "Does total points matter? I mean, what matters is head to head matchups— if our guys run faster than their guys in each race." With hopeful confidence he added, "I know we can beat Seacoast."

Stats looked down at the clipboard, flipping through the pages.

"You mean the Seacoast Wave?" asked Casey with a sly smile.

"Wave?" asked Tooch. "What wave?"

"They used to be the Seacoast Raiders," said Gil. "But they had to change their name. 'Raiders' was too violent."

"Like an ocean wave, wave?" asked Tooch.

"No. It's more like..." joked Casey raising his hand in the air, and waved. "Bye, bye, Seacoast."

Stats had lost interest in the coaches' results and handed the clipboard to Drew as if he were getting rid of an empty breakfast dish. "This team isn't going anywhere. You know what I'm saying? You're all running, for what?" he said, shaking his head. "There's just no point."

Recently Stats, along with Keith, had started to miss occasional practices. Unlike other sports where attendance was taken, indoor was looser. With just one coach and over thirty kids in different events, it was hard to keep tabs on the whole group.

Drew noticed though. He always kept a mental note of who was working out hard and should be taken seriously, and who was fading away and would be left behind. If Stats was missing training, he wouldn't be sharp for the meets. He was normally a five-pointer, and the team needed him to win his races in order to have a chance at a championship.

Keith was also a decent athlete but never showed any drive or determination to get faster, Drew thought. And Keith seemed to be heading in the wrong direction in life. Anyone who did business with Jeremy Lamonda had to be no good.

Stats, despite his tough-guy facade, was a bright and positive person. Drew felt that he had gotten to know Stats a bit and they got along well. There was a smart, confident guy inside Stats that was battling his way out. Drew wanted that guy to stay on his team, and started to think of a plan to keep Stats running.

Throughout that day's interval workout, Drew mulled the possibilities. He could talk to Stats about the missed workouts, but didn't think he had anything new to say that Stats hadn't already heard from him. He could have Coach Pilette intervene, but really, Coach wasn't much of a motivator or people person. If The Deuce knew about Stats missing practices he would probably just yell at him. But The Deuce wasn't a coach, and this wasn't football.

Walking back to the locker room with Gil, Casey, and Tooch, the idea finally came to Drew. He stopped in his tracks and said, "Tooch, you need a haircut."

"Maybe," a surprised and confused Tooch answered. "So?"

"So, you need to do it today," continued Drew. "I know the perfect barbershop. We can head there right after practice."

The guys had to take a city bus across town to get to Harold's American Barbershop. Since 1956 Harold Ranes had been cutting hair and making conversation at his corner shop. For the black men who lived and worked on that side of Aiken, Harold's American was an unofficial town hall meeting place. Usually there was more conversation than hair cutting going on in Harold's.

There were a few men conversing in the shop when the four runners opened the door and walked in. The boys weren't the normal clientele at Harold's, and at the sight of them, a Cambodian, Brazilian and two white kids, all conversation ceased to a deafening silence.

Harold, with his long experience of running a small business, filled the silence with a bright and warm welcome. "Well, look at these handsome young men," he announced to all the men in the shop. Then turning to the boys he said, "What can old Harold help you with this fine winter's afternoon?"

Drew stepped forward with a calm confidence that was sorely lacking in the other three. "My friend, Tooch," he said pointing to the smallest of his teammates, "needs a haircut."

"Looks like you all need a haircut, if you ask me," said Harold. The men in the waiting area gave a chuckle. "But since only one of you is paying, one haircut it will be."

Harold lifted his arm and held out his hand in front of him. The old man's unsteady hand wavered and shook in the air. "I'd say the days of Harold using scissors to give a cut have come and gone," Harold said, shaking his head. The men in the room murmured agreement. "Young Tooch here, needs a younger, steadier hand to do the job." Turning to the back of the shop Harold called out, "Clay! Got a customer for you."

With a gentle push from Drew, Tooch made his way to the barber's chair and settled in. Gil and Drew took the last two empty chairs in the waiting area. Casey, left without a chair, stood awkwardly next to a half empty coat rack.

When the younger barber, Clay Timlin, walked out of the back room and over to Tooch's chair, Drew smiled. This was the reason he pressured Tooch into getting a haircut on this side of Aiken. Clay Timlin was Stats's uncle.

Monique had told Drew about Uncle Clay and that Stats lived only with his mother. She also knew that Stats's dad had not been in the picture for a long, long time. Over the years Uncle Clay had stepped in and been the guiding hand in Stats's life. Uncle Clay, Drew thought, could get Stats back to indoor full time.

Clay Timlin was a tall and muscular man. His years in the US Army gave him an imposing and stern demeanor. Drew got the feeling that no one messed around with Mr. Clay Timlin. As he started in on Tooch's haircut, Clay asked, "How do you boys all know each other?"

"We are all on the indoor track team at Aiken High," answered Drew.

"No basketball?" asked Clay.

"No sir," answered Drew respectively. "Tooch and I run the mile, these guys," he said pointing to Gil and Casey, "run the two mile."

"Two mile?" repeated one of the men in the waiting room. "Grab the keys to the car for two miles!" he joked. The other men laughed. The runners did not. They've all heard that one before.

"We're on the team with Donell Timlin," offered Drew.

Clay stopped mid-scissor-cut, and for the first time smiled.

"Who?" asked a confused Casey, and then received an elbow to the thigh from Gil.

"Donell's running sprints?" asked an impressed Clay.

"Yes, he is one of the best in the state," declared Drew. "We actually have a really strong team this year, and Donell..." he said using Stats's real name and looking at Casey, "wins a lot of races and scores a lot of points for us."

"He's a hell of a football player," said one of the men.

"Broke the school record for rushing yards," added another.

"Now, is that your sister's son?" asked Harold.

"No. no," replied Clay. "Donell's my brother's, God rest his soul. Left behind a fine young man though." Clay beamed with pride. "Donell sure has the skills," he said. "With the football, and that boy's smarts, he could be playing at college next year." The men murmured agreement.

As Tooch's hair was being snipped to the floor, the haircut was coming into shape, and it looked surprisingly good. Drew realized this was the moment for his big pitch. He paused for a moment to collect himself.

"Well, we're on the indoor track team, and we have a very good team this year. In fact, our coach believes we are contenders for the state championship," said Drew.

The men all nodded, listening carefully. The mention of Coach Pilette drew skeptical looks from Casey and Gil. Coach had never said such a thing.

"To do that..." continued Drew. "To be the best, we need all of the guys on our team to give 100% all season long."

"That's right!" said Harold. "True enough," said Clay. The men all agreed.

"But, unfortunately," said Drew, getting ready to drop the bomb. No one likes a tattletale, and if Stats found out he was ratted out by his co-captain he might be pissed off. Stats was stronger and tougher, and there was a chance he would punch out Drew for telling on him. But the team needed Stats if they were to have any chance, so Drew gambled it was worth the risk. "It seems that Donell may be quitting the team."

The scissors stopped snipping Tooch's hair. Clay Timlin's smile had disappeared, his dark steely, US Army eyes focused sharply on Drew, and he asked, "Come again?"

A bead of nervous sweat formed on Drew's forehead under the glare of Mr. Timlin. "Ah, yes, sir. Well, you see," he stammered. "He hasn't been showing up to practice too much lately, and, uh…"

Harold's American Barbershop grew awfully quiet. For the first time Drew could hear the rattle of the heating vent along the wall. Casey uncomfortably shifted his weight from one leg to another.

Mr. Clay Timlin straightened up to his full height and took a step toward Drew. In a clear, purposeful, and forceful voice he said, "Oh, let me tell you one thing, Mister Drew Declan. Donell Timlin is going to be running sprints this winter for Aiken High. He will be at every practice, every meet, and I'll personally make sure he wins every damn race. Do you know what I'm saying?"

Old Harold let out a whoop to break the tension. "It's about time this town had a team win a state championship!" he said. To the laughter of the men in the shop he added, "And sounds like young Donell Timlin is going to lead the way!"

It was always the long runs—seven miles or more—when Drew did his best thinking. Even though there was adrenaline and dopamine flowing through his brain when he ran interval workouts, not one profound or reflective thought had ever come to him then. The long, repetitive movement—stride after stride for mile upon mile—had a meditative effect that brought calmness and clarity to his mind.

Drew set out by himself on a Sunday afternoon for an eight-mile route that followed the Nantuc River out of Aiken and into the neighboring town. With two layers under his jacket, pants, a winter hat and good gloves, the thirty-degree weather wouldn't bother him a bit. The morning snow showers had given away to sleet and then to a light rain, so for the first mile or so he had to squint and continuously wipe the rain off his face. Running in bad weather was just part of being a runner in New England. In fact, the worse the weather, the more pride he felt. It showed how tough he was. Basketball players don't run outside in the winter cold, but real runners could handle any conditions.

About three and a half miles into it he was warmed up and finally able to work through some of the stuff he had been thinking about lately. The indoor team was getting stronger each week. Coach Pilette, despite being preoccupied with his wife's pregnancy, was still coming up with workouts that were getting the guys into shape. Drew had never realized how bad Coach Morrissey had been until Coach Pilette showed him what a competent and motivated track coach was like. Pilette even spent time with the field event guys, helping the shot putters with their footwork and Asher with a proper approach to the bar. It was amazing how few injuries the team had. The extra stretching and exercises Coach installed in their workouts kept them healthy. The River Hawks had been soundly defeating their opponents in dual meets and they looked to get stronger as they headed toward the end of the regular season.

Drew was still troubled every time the short school bus pulled up to The Nest and Jeremy arrived. There had been a quiet, simmering truce between them since their interval battle. Neither one spoke to or even looked at the other. The story of their competition had made its way through the school's rumor mill, and word had gotten back to Jeremy about how he had "lost" to Drew and the team's little victory celebration. That made Jeremy seethe. Drew sensed that pent up anger, and worried that they may come to blows. With a runner's thin, light body type, he was not made for a fist fight. Jeremy's build was thicker and much stronger.

The dread of being beaten up had been on his mind, agitating his thoughts for days, and it made going to practice stressful. This long run calmed his mind and helped him see the situation in a new light. Jeremy, Drew realized, was a danger more to himself than anyone else. If he threw one punch, or even said the wrong thing to the wrong person, he'd be bounced out of the Aiken High athletic program, and that short bus would never show up again. Drew didn't have to do a thing. Just wait it out and Jeremy would implode on his own.

The tension and anxiety that had been plaguing him was washed away by the steady pace, rhythmic breathing, and fresh air of a long winter's run.

Another satisfying thought was the successful return of Stats to the team. Whatever Uncle Clay said to Stats worked. Drew wasn't sure if Stats knew about his visit to Harold's American Barbershop and since Stats never mentioned it, neither would he.

He did ask Stats about his dad. He remembered Clay saying that his brother would "rest his soul," and that he had "left behind" a son. At first Stats was suspicious of Drew's question, but after he realized that Drew was just trying to be sympathetic, he talked about his dad's death a little. It wasn't a long conversation, but it was significant. Kids only talk about important things like that with people they trust. It seemed that Stats, the black son of a single parent from the housing project, and Drew, the white son of two white-collar parents, were becoming friends.

It was amazing, Drew thought, that the guys on the team had come from so many different backgrounds, and still managed to be teammates and maybe even friends.

Take Theo Marshall, for example. His dad owned T.M. Replacement Windows, a successful home improvement business. Theo was probably the wealthiest guy on the team. Theo had nice clothes, his parents drove new cars, and they always flew to Florida during the winter school break.

Gil's parents were immigrants and lived in a rented apartment near the city center. As it turned out, Gil's dad worked for Theo's dad as a window installer. When Drew told Theo that his tough-guy persona affected Gil differently than everybody else, Theo was shocked. He had no idea who worked for his dad, and couldn't have cared less. With a little prodding from Drew, Theo struck up a conversation with Gil, and they found that they had a lot more in common than either had ever imagined. They weren't best friends by any stretch, but both guys could hang around together and were cool with being teammates.

Casey had two sets of parents since both of his parents remarried after their divorce. He called himself a ping-pong kid because he lived in two houses, shuffling back and forth depending on the week or weekend. There were times he had shown up to a meet without his uniform or racing shoes because he had left them at the other parent's house. At track, Casey was always cracking jokes and full of fun, but his home life was darker. There was a lot of distrust and animosity between his parents, and he was still exposed to some nasty and bitter fights. When running, Casey was free of the anger that permeated his family life, and his confident good humor flowed among his friends. His running buddies were more than just teammates, they were the gateway to living a happy life.

There was a large extended family of parents, brothers, sisters, cousins, and grandparents behind Tooch. All of them were immigrants from Cambodia, and many of them worked in the family restaurant, Heng Khmer. Coming out for cross country and track was one of the few times Tooch left the safe confines of his family circle and did something on his own.

As the last mile of his run cruised by, it became clear in Drew's mind that despite their different backgrounds the guys on the team could still be connected. Their identity didn't have to be defined by where they had come from, but what they now could do together. Being on a high school team may be a small thing compared to some of the things the guys had gone through in their lives so far, but it seemed to matter to them.

Drew slowed down and stopped in front of his house. His body was warm against the winter cold, and steam rolled off his neck and back. The late afternoon sun, peeking through the gap between the clouds and the horizon had turned the entire atmosphere an unbelievable orange and pink. Drew was so happy to be outside and experiencing the light. Despite the long effort he was still feeling strong and fluid. His mind was calm and confident. In his heart he knew that running on the team, and keeping the River Hawks together, was important work. He was going to make sure that nothing was going to stop them from winning.

His calm confidence was put to the test the next day during chemistry class. Science labs worked in groups of four, and in the past Drew had been stuck with people who either didn't do their share of the work, or were just annoying to work with. So he was relieved to see that Monique, his friend and confidant, was part of his group. Not only was Monique fun to talk to—she knew the best gossip in the school—she was a good student and would actually do her share of the work. They often tried to get on the same group projects because they would get a good grade working together.

It was when he learned that Shelley and Linda McKinnon were also in his lab group that Drew's confidence waned. Despite having a lot in common with them—running, classes, mutual friends, and so on—Drew never seemed to think of anything to say when he was near either one of them. Maybe, he hoped, this was a good chance to talk to them, get to know them a bit, and see if either one had any interest in him.

The sisters approached the lab table in full conversation, barely noticing their two new lab partners. ". . . and the faucet was one of those old ones, with the cold on one side and the hot on the other," said Shelley.

"Like, at the YMCA pool locker room, last summer?" Linda offered. "They should update them."

"There is way too much chlorine in that pool. I swear my hair turned green from all of that," said Shelley.

"Or, like the sink in grandma's basement, near the washing machine," said Linda. "I don't think there is much chlorine there. Smells like old clothes."

"Why update them?" said Shelley. "Her basement isn't that bad."

"Green's not a good hair color, even on St. Patrick's Day," said Linda. "You know, I think they are open all year long now."

"I think the dryer is the one that smells," said Linda. "The best ones let you control the temperature with one knob."

"It wasn't too green, I guess," said Shelley. "Smelled more like rags than clothes."

The onslaught of words derailed Drew's plan. How could he join a conversation that consisted of random sentence fragments? Monique, who recognized Drew's uncomfortableness for what it was, took no pity on him. "Drew, do you know Shelley and Linda," she asked in a mocking introduction. As if explaining the most simple thing to a small child, she added, "They are sisters."

The McKinnon's seemed to take Monique's words at face value, not comprehending the sarcasm. They knew who Drew was and didn't think they needed an introduction.

Drew tried to fill the ensuing silence. All he could come up with was, "Ah, hi."

Monique stifled a laugh.

Mr. Peterson, the balding, middle-aged science teacher wore the same plaid shortsleeve shirt and black tie every day of the week. "All right people. Let's stop talking and start this period by getting your lab trays out," he announced. Mr. Peterson did not have a sense of humor, and he ran a strict class. He was quick to send any misbehaving students to the office for detention.

Drew wanted to start a conversation with Shelley or Linda, but the only thought running through his mind was that there were no thoughts running through his mind. It was a never-ending feedback loop of nothing.

"People, remove the cover of your lab tray and set it aside," commanded Mr. Peterson. "We will dispose of the covers at the conclusion of the lesson." He slowly walked up and down the aisles of the classroom inspecting and finding fault with each group. "We do not want tray covers interfering with our work, do we?" Not hearing an answer from the students he said in a louder, more demanding voice, "Do we?"

The students grumbled out a monotone, lifeless reply, "No, Mr. Peterson."

Without any words in his brain to start a conversation Drew decided that action was necessary to impress the girls. He would dispose of the lab tray cover right now. He grabbed his cover, held it like a frisbee, and flung it past the faces of Shelley and Linda toward the tall trash barrel at the front of the class. The tray whipped through the air, slicing the gap between the two girls seated in front of them, and made a wide left hand arc for the barrel. But he had misjudged the distance, or maybe, since he had never thrown a lab tray cover before, he misjudged its weight. Either way, the tray's flightpath rapidly lost height and didn't have a chance of going in the barrel.

The clang of the plastic projectile hitting the stationary aluminum cylinder rang out across the classroom, bringing everyone to silence. Shelley and Linda had looks of utter shock on their faces. Monique, with an incredulous frown, simply asked the unanswerable question, "Why?"

"Excuse me?" started Mr. Peterson, who had turned around with the noise of the impact. Walking over to Drew he said, "This is room B317, Mr. Declan. We do not..." and he paused here to let the drama sink in, "throw objects across the room. Maybe when you are playing basketball or baseball—on a field— it would be appropriate, but here in room B317 it is decidedly not."

Realizing the magnitude of his impulsive stupidity, Drew's face felt flush with heat. All the students in the class were focused on him. His actions were definitely a conversation starter, but in quick hindsight, not the kind of conversation he had hoped for.

"The trash barrel in room B317 will not be dinged, dented, scratched or otherwise defaced," continued Mr. Peterson. His tone of voice had taken on an over-the-top, holier-than-thou tone. "You will make your way to the office, Mr. Declan. It's a point of personal pride for me that in room B317 the trash barrel will always be unblemished."

Aiken High's main office was a bright and open room where the secretaries had a commanding view of every student in the school's front hallway. Adjacent was a windowless, closet-sized room that served as a holding area for students awaiting discipline. With six seats, three on each side facing each other, there was little room for a backpack, textbook, or even the students' feet. Drew had never been to the holding room before, but he had heard stories of kids waiting in there, cramped up for hours. He hoped his lack of past discipline would help him avoid any detention, but he realized that throwing stuff across the classroom, even if it was just heading to the trash barrel, was an act that would not escape punishment. How much practice time would he have to miss, he wondered. Hopefully it would be on a day of an outdoor run, and he could just do the run by himself later in the day.

Already in the holding room were Stats and his cousin Keith. Drew and Stats were surprised to see each other, and acknowledged each other with a nod. Keith, who had quit the indoor team around the time of the hair cut conversation, had nothing to say to Drew, and neither boy even made eye contact.

"What are you here for?" asked Drew.

Stats shrugged his shoulders and said, "Slept late. Snooze-snooze." Then he added, "Tardy. How about you?"

"I, ah…" stumbled Drew. "I threw a tray cover across Mr. Peterson's class." Seeing Stats's eyebrows raise in surprise he added, "I was trying to throw it in the barrel, but I was a little short."

Stats laughed, and even Keith had to hide a smile. "You've never been famous for your eye-hand coordination," said Stats.

Drew settled in for what he thought was going to be a long, boring stay in the holding room. He closed his eyes, tilted his head back, and started to think of what a fool he made of himself in front of the McKinnon girls. After that display, he would never have a chance to date either one of them. And Monique would make fun of him forever.

Somehow the sisters were less interesting to him than they had ever been. Their mindless conversation about—what was it about? Socks in their grandmother's basement? None of it made any sense to him. And their obvious confusion with Monique's joke made them seem like they weren't the sharpest spikes on the racing flat. They didn't have Monique's sharpness or sense of humor. It was fun to talk to Monique. She could always keep a conversation going. In fact, he thought, rather than spend time with the clueless and vapid Shelley or Linda, he would rather spend his time with. . .

The door to the holding room opened and a teacher Drew had never seen before leaned into the room. "Mr. Timlin. Mr Declan. Both of you come this way," she ordered.

"Me too?" asked Keith.

"No," she said as if answering a trick question. "The word 'both' indicates two, not three, doesn't it?" Then she walked out of the room with Drew and Stats in tow, leaving Keith behind.

| 14 |

Within the Aiken Public Schools bureaucracy, there were many different factions competing for the limited funds city taxes provided. Each group championed their department's mission, which they believed was paramount to providing the best education possible to the students in their charge. During the financial allocation process, every department fought to increase their slice of the pie. The computer science department needed modern equipment to stay abreast of society's rapidly changing technology. With so many English as a second language students, the student resource center needed additional staff. The athletic department, the pride of Aiken High, pushed for more ice time at the city's hockey rink.

No other group or individual had more success at promoting their mission, working the system, and increasing their budget than the PRISM program, and its director Mrs. Roberta Drain.

While her diminutive stature was not imposing, her direct demeanor and sheer persistence cut through the red tape and budgeting problems that plagued other departments. Year after year, Mrs. Roberta Drain got the money, classroom space, and human resources to educate the most vulnerable and difficult students in the Aiken school district. The PRISM program was her life's work, and she was committed to her students. The program succeeded because of her determination and tenacity.

Getting her students out of the separate PRISM school and into Aiken High was a top priority of Mrs. Drain. She firmly believed that these children could only thrive if they participated in the same educational experiences as the rest of the students at Aiken High. But she met serious resistance from the Aiken High staff who feared the PRISM students may be too disruptive. They had, after all, been kicked out of the normal schools for just cause. While she had yet to place any of her students into Aiken High classrooms, for the first time she made progress when one of her students was allowed to join an Aiken High varsity team.

Mrs. Drain had seen her opportunity when the longtime track coach Mr. Morrissey retired, and a new coach had not been hired yet. She threw herself into that administrative vacuum, secured the funding for a minibus and driver, and placed Jeremy Lamonda on the roster of the River Hawks' indoor track team. She would build on the success of Jeremy, get more athletes onto the teams, and ultimately more PRISM students into the classrooms of Aiken High School.

Calling Jeremy a success story, however, was far from a sure thing. Reviewing his case, Mrs. Drain noted that he had made great strides in his emotional and behavioral health, but he had yet to develop any friends—or connections of any kind—with his teammates. More troubling was the rumor circulating the student population about a conflict with one of the team's captains, Drew Declan. If Jeremy's participation with the team was viewed as anything less than a success by the Aiken High staff and students, then the future of Mrs. Drain's PRISM program would be in jeopardy.

So it was another stroke of good luck for Mrs. Drain when she learned that two of the indoor track team's captains, including the Declan boy, were sitting together in the detention holding room.

"Gentlemen, you are in serious trouble," began Mrs. Drain when she sat the boys down in her office. "This may be the end of your athletic careers in high school."

Drew's mouth opened in shock. Could this be true? It was the first time he had ever been sent to the office in nearly four years of high school. How could one small incident kick him off the indoor team?

Stats frowned his eyebrows at Mrs. Drain's comment. He was suspicious. No one had ever been kicked off a team for tardiness before. Having grown up in the tough housing development, he had developed a sense when people were bluffing, and right now he felt Mrs. Drain was bluffing. "That's not right," he said.

"Oh, yes it is," countered Mrs. Drain, continuing her hard line. "It would take an extraordinary commitment from you both to maintain your athletic eligibility."

"Wait, what?" blurted Drew who was still stunned. "You can't kick us off the team."

"Oh yes I can," Mrs. Drain said in a cold voice. "I see only one way out of this unfortunate situation you have put yourself in, and as I said, it will take an extraordinary commitment on your part."

"What is exactly that commitment you're talking about?" asked Stats. He realized that Mrs. Drain's tough talk about losing athletic eligibility was a hard bargaining tactic, and he wanted to find out what she really wanted from them.

Mrs. Drain was quiet for a moment then changed to a softer demeanor. "You boys have an extraordinary hold on the other members of your team. I believe you have to do a better job of making all the other boys feel welcomed, and part of the group."

Drew was slow to pick up the bargaining that was going on and was still defensive. "What do you mean? We're different guys, but we are all good teammates."

"I'm still waiting for the commitment part," said Stats coolly.

"There is one member of the team that needs extra..." Mrs. Drain paused to find the right word, "friendship." She continued, "And I expect you to include him in any team social activities."

"Who's that?" demanded Drew.

Mrs. Drain didn't change her expression one bit, and answered, "Jeremy Lamonda."

"Whoa! The kid that always grabbing at his crotch?" said Stats.

"That's crazy," exclaimed Drew. "He's a jerk. He insults everyone. The girl's team can't stand him. The only person he talked to was..." He trailed off thinking of Keith, who was off the team and would probably drop out of school soon.

"And he's racist," said Stats in a slow, cool voice.

That caught Mrs. Drain off guard, and for the first time she seemed to lose her composure. "That is a serious charge, Mr. Timlin. It is inappropriate to defame others with unsubstantiated accusations."

"So, you're saying that we have to play nice with this guy, or you will pull our athletic eligibility. That's what you're saying, right?" said Stats.

Drew spun his head and looked at Stats in shock. He sounded more like a lawyer brokering a settlement than a poor kid from the Aiken Housing Development. Drew had never heard him speak with such confidence.

Mrs. Drain slowly nodded her head and said, "Athletic eligibility is reserved for students who do not have disciplinary problems, and you two are..."

Stats cut her off mid-sentence. "That's not good enough. The kid is racist," he said, repeating his biggest bargaining chip. "And, if you take us off the team, then who is going to be his buddy?"

Folding her arms across her chest, Mrs. Drain leaned back in her chair to reassess the situation.

"Without us, who are you going to blackmail to be all brotherly love with him? Big Theo?" asked Stats. "No. His dad donates too much money to mess with," he said, answering his own question. Then turning to Drew he asked, "Who's that little Asian kid who is always following you around?"

"Tooch?" Drew answered unsurely. "He's Cambodian." It was all starting to come clear to him that he wasn't in a high school detention meeting, but a negotiation between the two teammates and a powerful opponent.

"Oh, yeah," said Stats dripping with sarcasm. "Mr. Bigot Lamonda is just gonna snuggle up with a Cambodian refugee."

"This is not blackmail," said Mrs. Drain. "I have to ensure the conduct of all student athletes meets the department's code of cond..."

"You should call it 'whitemail', because you all are white," interrupted Stats with a charge that seemed to rattle Mrs. Drain. Then switching back to lawyer mode he delivered his next blow. "We're going to need something more than a threat of detention to make this work."

Drew was impressed how Stats had so easily taken charge of the conversation.

"Boys!" interjected Mrs. Drain trying to keep the conversation on track and regain the upper hand. "All I'm suggesting is that you make Mr. Lamonda a bigger part of your team when you play your games."

Drew was indignant. "We don't play in games," he scoffed. "We run in meets!"

"And we aren't that much of a team, compared to football," added Stats.

Mrs. Drain let out a heavy sigh and continued on with her argument. "I'm not really in the position to be handing out incentives of any kind," she started. "But, I would be willing to give a good recommendation for a certain afterschool job."

"We don't want some job," said Stats. "What we want is..."

"Uniforms," broke in Drew.

It was Stat's turn to be shocked by his teammate's interruption.

Using his own best lawyer voice Drew said to Mrs. Drain, "You want him to be on a team. What the 'team' needs is new uniforms."

Mrs. Roberta Drain was in an unusual situation. Seldom had she gone into a meeting without walking away with what she wanted. These two boys had boxed her into a corner. The Timlin boy was right, if she threw them off the team then the success of her PRISM student was finished. The Lamonda boy would never make friends on his own. The job offer she had floated would have been very difficult to arrange. This uniform idea could be something that could save the situation.

"Uniforms are expensive," she said weakly, signaling her acceptance of the idea.

"Getting cash doesn't seem to be problem for you, Mrs. PRISM," said Stats.

"And running jackets," added Drew, sensing Mrs. Drain's weakness.

Stats brightened up and said, "Oh yeah. Adidas brand. With three white stripes down the arms!" With a big smile he added, "Those jackets are flash! You know what I'm saying?'"

With a big smile of his own Drew turned to Mrs. Drain and added, "And we need them by next week."

| 15 |

Just about all runners—all athletes really—hate stretching. Despite the proven medical research that shows greater flexibility increases performance and reduces injury, runners will do anything to avoid it. The easiest way to avoid team stretching was to show up late to practice.

Coach Pilette believed in the importance of stretching, before and after workouts, and had instituted a complete stretching requirement for each runner. That made sense to Drew, but he knew that most of the guys would try to find a way around the requirement. So once again he turned to Theo Marshall, the tallest and largest guy on the team to enforce attendance for the team stretches. Theo also hated stretching, but he liked bossing around and intimidating the smaller, thinner runners even more. Only the high jumper, Asher Dane, was allowed to avoid the team stretching because he actually did a more complete stretching routine on his own. Between Drew's positive and inspirational urgings, and the threat of violence from Theo, the rest of the team regularly lined up, and improved their flexibility as the season ground on.

On the infield of the Nissitissit Wild Cats gymnasium the River Hawks boys indoor team gathered for the next regular season meet. This week, Drew and Theo had little problem rounding up the guys for the warmups and stretching. Even though it was fairly warm inside the gymnasium, every member was still wearing their brand new, red-and-black River Hawks running jackets. The new logo didn't have the bird's head or wings, just the talons clenching the word "River." The guys liked how they looked in the jackets individually, and they liked how they looked in their jackets together. Against the normal scene of mismatched sweat tops, singlets and shorts that the Wild Cats were dressed in, the new River Hawks looked like a united and powerful team.

Coach Pilette had been pleasantly surprised when he got summoned to the athletic director's office and informed of the new uniforms. He was new to the school and although getting uniforms mid-season seemed a bit unusual, he hadn't questioned his team's good fortune.

The school's equipment manager, The Deuce, was much more skeptical. The rush order for new uniforms had caught him by surprise, and in his haste he mistakenly purchased two sets of boy's uniforms rather than the appropriate style for the girl's team. Ms. DeLuca's team would have to wait another week for the delivery of their share of the windfall.

Having spent years thick in the Aiken High bureaucracy The Deuce was astounded how fast the administration appropriated the funding, confirmed the order, and secured a one week delivery. No team, not even the football team, had ever received new uniforms in the midst of a season. And where, The Deuce wondered, did the funding for these uniforms come from? Certainly not from his part of the athletic department's budget. Who had the clout to get it done, and so quickly? The Deuce mulled the possibilities.

The new coach, Pilette? No. He was meek as a mouse and could barely keep a practice organized. On top of that the guy was a bundle of nerves with his wife expecting so soon.

Marshall the shot putter? His dad owned the big window replacement company that was always advertising on the sports radio station. Family money could get something like that done, but they would have sprung for new football helmets, or something important, not track uniforms.

What about that pesky runner Declan, The Deuce pondered. He was always wheeling and dealing. Things seemed to get done when he was around. He wouldn't shut up about how the indoor team was going to win the championship. And with such an inexperienced and weak coach, the kid practically ran the team.

Before the indoor team boarded the buses to the Nissitissit meet, The Deuce pulled Drew aside in the underground hallway. "How did you do it—get the new uniforms?" he grumbled at Drew.

Drew raised his eyebrows in surprise and tried to deflect the question. "I don't know what you are talking abo…"

"Don't give me that," interrupted The Deuce. Like a cop interrogating a perpetrator he leaned into Drew. "It was you, wasn't it? You're taking money away from other teams, you know. Some other team isn't going to get stuff because of this."

The accusation of taking money away from other athletes at Aiken High hurt Drew. "That's not true," he blurted. "PRISM would never buy anyone else uniforms."

Now it was The Deuce's turn to be surprised. "PRISM?" he asked, loosening his grip on Drew's arm. That Drain lady had an iron fist on the PRISM program, and she had plenty of money in her budget, he thought. But how did this kid pry loose funds from the toughest and most powerful bureaucrat in the school district? "You got money from Drain? That lady doesn't give up money easily."

Drew started to stammer out another denial. "I didn't get money from anybody..."

"You know what that is, kid?" interrupted The Deuce again. Before Drew could reply, The Deuce answered his own question. "Impressive."

Pulling Drew back into the center of the hallway The Deuce ended the conversation. "Now get on that bus and win your team the game."

"It's a meet, not a game," corrected Drew.

The Deuce jokingly balled up a fist and added, "Don't mess with me, River Hawk. Just go run."

The Nissitissit Wild Cats had a few decent runners on their team, but their squad lacked depth, and Drew predicted they couldn't possibly score enough points to beat the River Hawks. Normally he would have worried that his teammates might relax their guard and not run so hard against an inferior team, but the new uniforms had everyone pumped up for their race. They were ready to burst out and roll past the Wild Cats.

Coach Pilette took a long time getting off the bus. He had been distracted earlier in the day and hadn't completed the paperwork for the meet. Alone on the bus, he used the quiet time to finalize the roster. By the time he reached the track his team had completely finished their warmups. Preoccupied with submitting the roster to the meet officials, he was oblivious to the team's charged up attitude and readiness to race.

What his team needed at this moment, Coach Pilette believed, was a pep talk. In the previous four meets, and all of the practices for that matter, Coach Pilette had never come close to providing his team with inspiration. He was great with describing the science behind the workouts and race tactics, but any kind of social communication from the coach was awkward and uninspiring.

"Team," he began after the captains had rounded up most of the guys, "we need to keep our focus. Because when we have focus…" He paused, searching for a conclusion to the analogy, "we're not running blind. When we run blind we can't see. And we need to see."

Usually when Coach Pilette talked to the team most of the guys tuned him out knowing that Drew would come around later and tell them what they really needed to know. But this talk was worth paying attention to only because it was entertainingly awkward.

"When we see well, we will run fast," continued Coach. "But it is more than just seeing. It's keeping track of your pace. And the other runners. It's an intensity more like…" Once again Coach paused, searching for a finish.

"Focus?" offered Casey with a sly smile.

"Right!" said Coach, pointing his finger at Casey. "Yes, you got it! Focus! With focus we can see, and win."

"Hey Coach," interrupted Gil. "I don't get it. What are we supposed to focus on?"

Nodding his head as if he were a preacher in front of a congregation of true believers, Coach responded, "Oh, I think you know. Yes, you know. When you stop and get focus, you'll see what focus can do."

"Wait," said Casey. "We're supposed to stop? I thought we were supposed to run."

"Run with focus!" continued Coach Pilette. Winding up to what he hoped would be a big finish he abruptly switched metaphors, "And with that, we will swing for the fence!"

The team was silent, lost in confusion. "You mean, like, with a baseball bat?" asked Gil. The three shot putters, having seen that none of this applied to them, turned and walked away from the meeting.

"Should we bring bats to the next meet?" joked Casey. More guys started leaving the meeting.

Seeing that the scene was quickly devolving Drew stepped forward, held out his hand and said, "Ok guys. River Hawks on three." The remaining teammates put their hands on top of his, shouted the team's nickname, then got ready to run.

The meet went better than Drew could have imagined. The River Hawk runners were in better shape and more motivated than any other team he had been on. Stats, Constantine, Drew, and Casey all scored five points when they won their races. The shot putters swept and Asher easily cleared the winning height.

Their win in the final race of the meet, the 4x440 relay, just padded the River Hawks margin of victory.

Only one runner underperformed and raced poorly, Jeremy Lamonda. He was sluggish in his race, faded noticeably over the last lap and a half, and finished fifth. After crossing the finish line he doubled over in obvious pain, putting his hands where he so often put them, over his crotch.

Stats apparently never had any intention of living up to his part of the deal with Mrs. Drain. Since the discipline meeting he had never spoken to or even approached Jeremy once. Drew reluctantly tried to talk to Jeremy twice, but both times he was greeted with a scowl and insult. Drew never bothered a third time, and tried to dismiss Jeremy from his mind, wishing that the SOB would simply go away. There was no way Mrs. Drain could find out how hard, or how little they tried to befriend Jeremy, and she wouldn't be able to take away their running jackets now.

The only thing that hung in Drew's mind was a question of athleticism. How did a naturally gifted athlete like Jeremy, who had hung with Drew stride for stride in that workout just a few weeks ago, become a weak and wilting runner? What could bring down an athlete like that in such a short period of time? On one hand, he disliked Jeremy and wanted to block any thought of him. On the other, there was obviously something curiously wrong with the jerk and that kept Jeremy Lamonda in his mind.

| 16 |

Workouts the day following a meet were generally lighter than most because Coach Pilette didn't want runners expending a maximum effort two days in a row. The promise of an easy workout and the good feelings of having won the meet had everyone in a light and easy mood.

Coach Pilette had Drew, Tooch, and the other milers staying indoors and working out with the middle distance runners. Gil, Casey, and the younger distance runners hit the road for an easy five miler. Theo and the Loganikos brothers went to lift in the football weight room. Stats, and the sprinters worked on their starting block technique, but mostly they stood around and joked with each other. Asher Dane rested comfortably on the high jump mat, deep in conversation with a few of the girl high jumpers. After he gave out the workouts and saw that things were under way, Coach Pilette slipped out of The Nest early to get to his wife's next birthing class.

Coach Pilette's lame motivational speech had the team laughing since the meet. The line about "swinging for the fence" in particular, was too good to let go. It was worked into every conversation. "I'll have a burger, fries, soft drink, and then SWING

FOR THE FENCE!" mocked Casey to gales of laughter from the guys.

"Let's go on an easy five miler..." joined in Gil, "and SWING FOR THE FENCE!"

Later someone, no one could remember who, suggested that they actually run the five miles with real bats, and, of course, "SWING FOR THE FENCE." Before the distance runners took off they stopped by the athletic department's equipment room, and when no one was looking, grabbed about seven aluminum bats.

In the corner of the equipment room was a bin full of old, discarded uniforms that were in such bad shape The Deuce refused to hand them out to current teams. Rummaging through the bin a few guys found remnants of Aiken High baseball shirts. If they were going to swing for the fence, they reasoned, they might as well wear baseball shirts. Deeper into the bin they found older, more eclectic uniforms with long abandoned River Hawk logos. A swim team sweat top from the 1970s with a fish logo. Collared polo shirts from a long forgotten tennis team. A woolen football jersey straight out of the 1950s, which had to have been the kickers shirt because it had the number 3.

Their running jackets, brand new and just moments before so proudly worn, were unceremoniously tossed into the track locker room, and the distance runners set out on the roads looking like an unkept anthropological review of Aiken High sports fashion.

For the first mile or so they made snowballs from the roadside snowbanks and pitched them to the guys with the bats. Being runners, the pitching was poor and the swinging unsteady, but occasionally a bat would smash into a snowball, exploding in a flash of white.

Closing in on mile three they ran past a chain-link fence and discovered the cool sound the aluminum bats made when dragged along the steel wires. Tapping a stop sign with a bat made a cymbal-crash sound. Mailboxes, street signs, and fire hydrants each produced a unique, funny sound when given a little tap with an aluminum baseball bat.

The guys made their way across Aiken in the twilight of a February afternoon tapping and hitting any hard metallic or stone surface with the bats.

Around mile four they had run out of things to hit that wouldn't break, and the joke was losing its steam. The bats were starting to feel heavy, and no one wanted to keep on carrying them for the last mile back to The Nest. They decided to stash the bats behind the restaurant Tooch's parents owned, and resolved to come back and get them the next time one of them could borrow a car.

By the time they returned to The Nest and started their post-run stretches, the "swing for the fence" jokes had been exhausted. The litter of old uniforms had been stuffed back into the equipment room bin, and conversation returned to the normal litany of topics, ranging from school and homework to TV shows and music. A heated debate broke out about whether the two Scottish singers who wrote "I'm Gonna Be" could possibly run 500 miles, let alone the 1,000 mile round trip. The bats had been forgotten like yesterday's news.

Back at The Nest, Drew's workout had been a breeze, a simple 220, 220, 440, 660 ladder. The pace had been comfortable and smooth.

The girl's team, who had also handily won their meet, were having an equally easy workout. As practice wound down, members of both teams were milling around and hanging out. Drew was going to congratulate Shelley and Linda on winning their races yesterday, but as he approached the girls he started to have second thoughts. In the past he would have found himself tongue-tied around the girls, and that would have been reason enough to avoid them. He was still a bit embarrassed about the whole trash can thing in science class, but that wasn't stopping him today. He was beginning to realize that every time he saw them they were involved in that constant, overlapping and in-coherent conversation. He could never get a word in because they filled up the air with their blathering. Who, he wondered, wanted to be around that?

Besides, their races were actually not that impressive. Medi-ocre times against inferior competition. The most impressive race for the girls team had been run by Shelley and Linda's younger sister, Mary. She ran a personal best time, and nearly passed Linda in the last few yards of the mile race. It occurred to Drew that she was going to get even faster and would soon be the best runner in their family.

Their dad, a state police detective, was an intimidating guy. Whenever Drew saw Mr. McKinnon at one of their meets he could see where the service revolver made a bulge under his sports coat. The state police badge attached to his belt was clearly visible. He stood tall and straight, his hair was always in a short buzz cut, and unless he was talking to one of his daughters, he did not smile. If Drew ever wanted to date one of the McKinnon sisters he would probably have to talk with Mr. McKinnon, and that was one more reason why Shelley and Linda were a little less interesting.

When Drew got home that afternoon Lazer, as usual, was the only one home to greet him. With his ears back and tail wagging, Lazer lumbered into the kitchen and leaned into Drew's leg. After Drew finished petting him, Lazer made three tight circles around where he was standing, then laid down and let out a heavy sigh. Just a moment later, Lazer was raising himself back to his feet when he saw that his master was done in the kitchen and heading for the staircase. Once in Drew's bedroom, Lazer found a comfortable spot, circled a few times, and laid down with another heavy sigh.

The two spent many afternoon hours together in the bedroom while Drew did his homework. Sometimes there would be music playing, other times it was so quiet Lazer could hear the pages of a book turning, or even the scratch of pencil on paper.

Today Drew was too distracted to get going on his homework, so he laid back on his bed, grabbed an old tennis ball off the floor and started tossing it into the air. Lazer watched the ball go up and down for a while, then dozed off.

At first Drew pondered the question of Shelley and Linda. For so long he had been interested in the girls, but he had never talked to them. Now that he knew them a little better, he didn't really want to talk to them. He'd much rather hang out and talk with Monique. He and Monique always had a good time joking around in the hallways of school, or on bus trips to meets. She was a good athlete, one of the top point scorers for the girls team. But. . .

But what? He wasn't interested in Monique like he had been with the McKinnons. Why, he wondered, was there a difference between the girls you liked, and the girls you like-liked?

Drew sat up quickly, startling Lazer. "Lazer," he said out loud to the dog. Lazer was now alert wondering if his master was going to take him for a walk. "Why can't there be a girl that you like, like-like," he paused trying to finish the thought, "and she feels the same way about you? Why not?"

Silence took over the room as Drew let this thought sink into his own head. Lazer, realizing that he wasn't going for a walk anytime soon, relaxed, put his head back down, and let out another heavy, heavy sigh.

| 17 |

The Aiken High School athletic department neatly divided their team sports into two categories, cut teams and non-cut teams. Any athlete trying out for the boys and girls varsity basketball team, for example, would either make one of the team's twelve varsity slots, or be cut. The cross country and track teams were listed as non-cut, where any student who signed up and practiced throughout season was allowed to run in the meets. On the surface this was true, but in practice the teams tried hard to weed out those who were not serious about running. The XC team's Gut Run usually eliminated a third of those who showed up for the first practice. And while it was true that anyone on the indoor team was allowed to get on the bus and run the regular season meets, to run in the important meet, the state meet where championships were decided, runners had to run a qualifying time or be left behind.

Qualifying times for the indoor track and field state championship were not easy to reach, and many towns only sent a handful of runners to the big meet. For many qualifiers the state meet was an opportunity to showcase their individual talent one last time, but their team's season was effectively over. Even if a runner won his event and became state champion, his team would only record those ten points, and have no chance to outscore the more powerful schools. To win a championship a team needed a deep roster of strong runners in multiple events. The points scored by the second, third, and down to the tenth place finisher of each event would add up and put their team in contention for the championship.

Drew wanted as many of his teammates as possible to qualify. The more guys on the River Hawks state meet team, the more points they could score. From the first day of practice he preached and promoted the importance of meeting the standard.

Early in the season many of the guys were indifferent to their qualifying times. For some, the state championship meet at the end of the season was too far off to focus on. Others secretly didn't think they had a chance to meet the requirement and showed indifference to hide their self doubt. Casey had joked that he would probably be on vacation by the first week of March. When Constantine heard the qualifying time for the hurdles, he paused for a long moment looking slack jawed, then scoffed, "Who cares? It's just track."

As the season went on the runners grew stronger, and one by one the athletes started to make the grade. On the wall of the locker room Drew posted the set of names of those who had qualified, and no one could walk in or out without seeing who was in the A Set, and who would be left behind.

Unlike other sports where the teacher's pet could make the roster over a better athlete, there were no coaches' decisions. The guys either ran the time, threw the distance, jumped the height, or they didn't. In indoor, each guy had to prove that they belonged in the championship meet.

The guys who hadn't made it yet took it as a hit to their pride. None of them wanted to be outside the A Set. Their desire to be on that list—the list of state contenders, the list of the real athletes in the school—grew. And the only way to get in the A Set was to work harder and get faster.

A few guys made the list easily, and were expected to score well in the state meet. Stats in the 50, Drew in the mile, Theo in the shot put. Surprisingly, the next guy to easily qualify was Asher Dane, the high jumper.

Asher never treated the high jump as a competition. He felt his fellow jumpers were all reaching for the same athletic enlightenment together. To reach up, roll and twist one's body in the air with precision, strength, and flexibility was, for him, more of a performance than sport. Each jump was an artistic expression of human motion rather than an act of athleticism. He once told Drew that the high jump was "an act of physical grace."

Drew never understood what Asher was talking about. Competition, Drew believed, was an essential part of life. It was about being the best and beating as many other runners as possible. When Drew raced other runners he wanted to turn up the pace and inflict as much pain as possible on his competitor. He wanted them to wither away in agony for even thinking they could race with him. He wanted to be the fastest, toughest runner he could be. He wanted to be the best. He wanted to win.

One thing he did understand about Asher was the guy could jump higher than anyone who had ever been on the team. If they had radically different viewpoints on what it meant to compete and how to approach life, so what? As long Asher could score points at the state meet then Drew was all for "acts of physical grace" too.

Casey and Gil were the next to qualify, both in the two mile. They had a friendly competition all season and had pushed each other in every training interval and race. Casey had a little more closing speed and would always try to hang onto Gil until the last lap, where he would unleash his kick and try to out sprint Gil to the finish. Gil had more strength and always pushed the pace early, hoping to break Casey. If he had a big enough lead on the last lap, he could usually hold off Casey's kick.

There were a few more guys that were close to qualifying, and the pressure was on to meet the standard in one of the few remaining regular season meets. Constantine was sure to qualify in the hurdles if he could ever run a clean race. He had a good start, enough speed, and clean form over the hurdles, but he had a hard time running the correct number of strides between hurdles. Novice hurdlers often ran five short choppy strides between hurdles, which was inefficient. The best hurdlers consistently three-stepped. Constantine, the goofball, four-stepped, alternating his lead leg over each hurdle. Inevitably, late in races, he would hit hurdles, lose his balance, and ruin his chance of running a fast time. Coach Pilette insisted that this season Constantine learn how to consistently three-step. A clean three-step race, Coach preached to him, was the only way to run a fast time and score at the big meet.

Lately Constantine had grown serious about practicing his three stride form. Coach Pilette had brought a video camcorder to practice and taped the hurdler's workout. In the school library Constantine got permission from the librarian to use the TV and VHS deck, and along with Coach reviewed his form and technique. It was normal for the Aiken High football team to watch game footage every week of their season, but this was the first time anyone had ever heard of a track team using film study.

The Loganikos brothers were also closing in on a qualifying distance in the shot put. They shadowed Theo in the weight room, trying to match him pound for pound in every lift session. Somehow their increased strength didn't translate into better throws. Coach Pilette believed that their extra effort in the weight room was leaving their arms fatigued, and maintained that tapering their lift sessions would give more life to their arms. He'd rather have them spend more time improving their footwork in the ring. The brothers were uncharacteristically divided on what to do. Mark insisted that strength equaled power, and continued lifting as much as he could to keep up with Theo. Michael listened to his coach, and tapered.

Sal Lombardo had just been kicked off the Aiken High basketball team for "violating team rules." The basketball coach, who according to the disgruntled players, was an overbearing control freak, had instituted a team rule requiring them to wear a collared shirt and tie to school on game days. Sal, insisting that the clothes he wore to school did not have any impact on his game, refused and was "made an example of." Drew knew that an excellent athlete like Sal would be a key addition to the indoor team, and quickly recruited him with the assurance that no track team in history ever had a dress code. On the season's final day of eligibility Drew had coach Pilette add the former basketball player to the indoor roster. JB, the basketball team's trainer was indignant at the defection, and playfully yelled, "Traitor!" at Lombardo every time they came across one another in the hallways. The nickname stuck, and now Traitor was a member of the indoor team.

In a blow to the egos of the veteran runners, Traitor ran a state qualifying time for the 600 in his first meet and made the A Set.

Tooch's ability to qualify was in question. The high mileage he ran for XC gave him plenty of strength, and in the early part of the indoor season he lowered his mile PR each week. He expected his times would keep on falling the more he trained, but by midseason his times had plateaued. Over the last few meets he neither improved or slowed. Maybe, like the Loganikos, his high mileage and strong workouts had created fatigue that sapped his speed. Having a head cold for the last week or so didn't help. The result was that Tooch, the kid who wanted to be part of the A Set more than anyone else, looked as if he would be left behind.

As the other guys earned their qualifying times, and bragged about how well they would do at the championship, Tooch burned with envy. In the years after his move to Aiken he had been the loneliest of outsiders. The new language and confusing customs made it hard to make friends. While other kids played together in the streets or practiced with their little league teams, Tooch sequestered himself in the kitchen of Heng Khmer with his grandmother. Outside of his family circle, he felt as if he was just a little kid with an unfamiliar name from a faraway place. When he joined the River Hawks and survived the Gut Run, he finally found a group that he could be part of. Accepted by all. A member of the team. No longer an outsider, he was comfortable, happy, and proud.

It was midway through his first outdoor season when Tooch realized that there was a smaller, more exclusive club within the team. It was a club of guys who were the best, who had separated themselves from the weaker, ordinary, and unremarkable athletes that filled out the roster. Their speed, power, and endurance had elevated them into the upper tier of athletes at Aiken High. They had proved they could win their races and were confident that they would win again. This club had no name or no formal rules of acceptance. Membership only became apparent when they commanded the respect of the other athletes in school.

Tooch feared that he couldn't run the time and would be left on the outside again. When he was younger and insecure, he would have just melted away and retreated into the safe confines of his family. Older now, he was determined not to retreat. He was going to take his fear, and turn it into resolve. He knew he could run faster. He belonged on the A Set, and there was not a single thing on this earth—not being an immigrant, not having to learn a new language, not being picked on by bigger kids—that was going to stop him from getting on the A Set. Tooch knew he could do it.

With the state meet roster filling up, Drew tried to calculate the point total the River Hawks could possibly score. Assuming each runner would match their best time at the state meet, and correlating that with the top times of other runners in the state, he could loosely project what place they might finish. But it was difficult to keep all the times and points straight in his head, so instead, he kept grilling Stats with questions.

Hanging around The Nest after practice one afternoon he cornered Stats. "All right, if you add in Traitor, and both Loganikos brothers, how many points are we looking at?" asked Drew.

Stats let out a heavy breath, shook his head, and flipped through the pages of the coaching reports. "You think Traitor can run that time again? That's crush," said Stats. "And both of those Greek geeks?"

"Yeah," said Drew, acknowledging the unlikeliness of what he had asked. "But just saying, how many points?"

"We're looking at about," said Stats pausing to do the calculations in his head. "Twenty-five or thirty."

"Wow," said Drew. It was a higher number than he had thought. Switching to a frown he demanded, "What about Seacoast? How many points can they score?"

Stats slumped his shoulders at the difficulty of the question. "What am I, the head Wave coach? Ask him."

"Come on," insisted Drew. "What can they score?"

Shuffling around the papers, Stats looked at the times of the top runners on the Seacoast Wave, and similarly projected their place and score. This type of calculation would normally take Drew an entire weekend to figure out. Stats's incredible recall of statistics and pure mathematical computation skill allowed him to come up with an answer in minutes.

The first few weeks after Drew learned of Stats's ability, he would secretly go back home and recheck the numbers just to make sure Stats wasn't making up answers. After finding Stats's numbers were spot on every time, he gave up the double checking and completely relied on his co-captain.

With his eyebrows raised in surprise Stats delivered his result. "They could score about twenty-three, maybe twenty-eight. It's close, and we are just guessing on the times, but we could win" he said. A silence fell over the guys standing around the group. If there had been any lingering doubt about their chance to win it all, it was wiped away with the mathematical certainty that Stats had just delivered. They had confidence. They believed. They were sure. The River Hawks were going to run to a state championship.

After showering and changing into his street clothes, Drew packed up his bag for the walk home. Just about all the other guys had to grab a bus across town to their neighborhoods, but Drew's house was within a mile of the high school. On these cold February afternoons with temperatures in the mid-20s his wet hair would freeze on the walk home, so he lingered in the locker room longer than usual waiting for his hair to completely dry. He was the last one left, and the room, which had been filled with the sounds of slamming lockers and guys joking around moments ago, was quiet. The dull sound of basketballs thumping on the floor above and the hum of fluorescent lights, normally background noise, filled the room. After a tough workout and the normal locker room raucous, the quiet helped Drew feel calm and serene.

Coach Pilette had lectured the team on the science behind strong exercise, specifically how the body releases endorphins into the brain, creating runner's high - that relaxing, peaceful state that makes all runners want to come back for their next run. Drew was enjoying the moment.

The sound of a smack and a yelp of pain from out in the hallway broke the peaceful mood. The smack sounded as if someone took a hockey stick and whacked a hollow tree trunk. Drew had heard that sound before, but couldn't place it. The yelp wasn't only one of pain, it also included a measure of fear.

Stepping out into the hallway Drew saw JB crouched over with his arms up, covering his head. The basketball team's water bottles rolled on the floor beneath his feet. Standing over JB, with his hands poised to strike again was Jeremy. "Stop!" pleaded JB.

It clicked in Drew's brain—the smack sound must have been Jeremy's knuckles rapping JB's scull. Jeremy had flicked Tooch's skull earlier in the season and the sound was the same. But today it sounded louder and more painful.

Jeremy jumped around the front of JB and reached in for another knuckle-flick on the forehead. The sound of his knuckle wrapping JB's skull rang out again. Jeremy laughed, feeling empowered by his dominance over a weaker, helpless victim.

Drew was normally a cautious thinker, someone who thought through problems, planned ahead and meticulously worked his way to reach his goals. Even in races, Drew would patiently stay on pace until the fire of competition pushed him on faster. But now, there were no thoughts in his head, just emotion. Outrage. Anger. Hate. The whole school loved JB and held him in a protective embrace. The sight of him being physically beaten was enraging. Blazing red hot anger filled Drew.

Dropping his bag, he threw his body at Jeremy, driving an elbow into the side of his head. The blow knocked Jeremy off JB's crouched body and into the wall of lockers. Drew followed up with a left handed punch to the head, but it missed, landing on Jeremy's collar bone. Free from Jeremy's grasp, JB bolted for the stairs up to The Nest. Jeremy recovered from the surprise of the first blows and regained his balance. Seeing that it was Drew Declan who had attacked him, Jeremy's face filled with a wild anger.

Drew realized that his long expected confrontation with Jeremy was happening right now. It wasn't at all like he had imagined. He was all alone in an empty hallway, up against a stronger and more powerful guy. Fear started to creep in. Jeremy could stand there and pummel him with no one to stop the beating. There was only one thing he could do, what he had trained himself to do for years; don't stop, turn it up, and keep on fighting. Drew swung out with his right fist to Jeremy's face.

Jeremy dogged, and the blow landed on his left ear. Regaining his balance he swung and landed a blow on Drew's forehead.

Stunned by the shot to his head, Drew stumbled back and dropped his arms to his waist. Seeing Drew defenseless, Jeremy wound up for a blow straight to Drew's face.

A girl's scream filled the hallway and Drew became aware that other people were watching the fight.

Just as his body shifted weight to deliver the punch, Jeremy winced in an awful pain, and doubled over, clutching both hands on his crotch.

Drew couldn't figure out what caused Jeremy to crumble, but he recognized this was his chance to gain the advantage. He put both hands around Jeremy's neck and drove his head into the lockers.

"Hey! Cut that out!" boomed a man's voice. The Deuce heard the commotion and had come out of the equipment room to investigate. Over his years of working with teenagers he had seen many fights, and knew that with their fully developed muscles, a fist fight could be seriously dangerous.

Drew stopped at the sound of The Deuce's commanding yell, but before he could step back he heard the pounding of a dozen feet coming down the stairwell. JB had told the guys on the basketball team about Jeremy's attack, and they bolted out of practice running downstairs to inflict revenge on Jeremy.

The Deuce, realizing that Jeremy was in danger of being pummeled by eleven angry teenagers, stepped forward and bellowed at the basketball team, "Stop right there!"

The authority behind the command slowed the guys, but since The Deuce was neither a teacher or coach they still moved forward toward Jeremy.

"Anyone who takes another step," boomed The Deuce, "will be kicked off the team, and you will have to forfeit all of your games."

The Deuce had found the one thing that could hold back infuriated teenagers. If Traitor could be kicked off the team for not wearing a tie, beating a guy in the school hallway would definitely end their basketball careers.

"Get back upstairs," The Deuce yelled. "Now!" Turning to Drew he said, "You. Grab your bag and go home. I'll deal with you later." Grabbing Jeremy by the arm he said, "You. I'm making sure you get on your damn bus. No one's getting killed on my watch."

A moment later the hallway was as empty and quiet as it had been a few minutes earlier, but that relaxing peaceful feeling Drew had was long gone. The adrenaline that had been pumping in his body during the fight was rapidly leaving. As he reached down for his backpack he noticed that his hands were shaking. His mind raced, replaying the events of the last few minutes. JB yelling in fear. The sound of Jeremy's knuckles on JB's skull. His punch that missed Jeremy's face and hit his ear. The basketball team, ready to kill Jeremy. The Deuce yelling to break it up, and then marching Jeremy off to his bus. And the scream. He had heard a girl's scream, hadn't he?

"Wow, that was so cool," said the girl. "You should have pounded him into the wall. No one likes him."

Drew turned to find one girl from the indoor team with him in the hall. It was Shelley and Linda McKinnon's little sister. With all the excitement that just went on, he couldn't remember her name. Marie? Meghan? "Were you the one who screamed?" he asked.

"Ha, yeah. I guess I did," she laughed. With a smile that acknowledged the truth she added, "For a second I thought he was going to punch your head off."

Realizing he was lucky that Jeremy didn't land that big punch he replied, "Me too." What caused Jeremy to crumple to his waist in pain, he wondered. Whatever it was, he was glad it saved him.

"I guess I didn't do a good job of it," he added. "I think I missed him every time I threw a punch."

"Are you kidding?" she said. "You saved JB. You stood up to that jerk. It was amazing!"

Mary. It finally came to him. Her name was Mary. His head must be clearing. They started to walk down the hallway to the exit.

"Just wait until the entire school hears about it," she continued excitedly. "You're going to be, like, a hero around here."

"The entire school?" he repeated. If the whole school heard about it, then teachers would hear about it. Fighting in school is serious, and he could get suspended. He could, he realized, get kicked off the indoor team!

"Don't tell anyone," he said. "Mary, I could get kicked off the team."

Mary raised an eyebrow. "Are you kidding me?" she said again. "The whole basketball team saw it. JB will tell everyone he sees for weeks." Then she added with another big smile, "Hey, you know my name. I didn't think you ever noticed me."

"Of course I know your name," he said indignantly. To be honest, besides watching her race, he had never really given Mary much thought. She was taller than he remembered. Her hair was blond like her sisters, but she wore it short and with some curls. She had a great smile. "You had some really good races this season."

"Thanks."

They walked together in silence for a moment.

"I have science with Shelley and Linda," Drew began. "They never talk about you."

"Ha!" laughed Mary. "Then I must be the ONLY thing they don't talk about." Raising her hand and making a hand puppet she mocked her sisters, "Bla, bla, bla." Raising her other hand into a second hand puppet she started a conversation between the two hands. "Bla, bla, bla?" asked the left hand. "Bla, bla, bla!" answered the right hand.

Drew let out a big laugh. He was smiling ear to ear. A few minutes ago he had been in a fighting rage, then shaking with shock after the fight, but now, walking and talking with Mary he was back to being relaxed and having fun. What a crazy afternoon, he thought.

"Hey," said Mary reaching up to Drew's forehead. "You're not going to be keeping any secrets with this bruise on your forehead. Does it hurt?" she asked with concern.

He wasn't expecting her touch. Growing up, his family was not really touchy-feely. There were very few hugs, or pats on the back. Not that he wasn't loved by his parents, just that they never expressed it physically. Hugs from his aunts at Thanksgiving and Christmas were always awkward and uncomfortable. Mary's touch surprised him with how good it felt.

"Naw," he said. "I'm all right."

"Yeah," agreed Mary.

They had reached the end of the hall and paused before heading out into the cold winter weather.

"My dad is picking me up," said Mary. "Do you want a ride home?"

Drew remembered how intimidating Mr. McKinnon was, and briefly wondered if he had his service revolver with him even when he was picking up his daughters at school. "No thanks. I'm ok walking home."

"Right," said Mary, hiding a little disappointment. "Maybe next time."

"Maybe," agreed Drew with a smile.

They left the building and went their separate ways. Drew inhaled in a deep breath of cold air and let it out slowly. He needed the time on the walk home to think through all the ramifications of today's events. Would he have to have another fight with Jeremy? What would The Deuce say to him? Would he get suspended for the fight, and get kicked off the team? And when could he hang out with Mary again?

| 18 |

Theo Marshall had never been in trouble at school. He had never skipped a class, never arrived after the first bell, and had never been sent to the office by a teacher. No one ever tried to start a fight with him because his large muscular frame intimidated even the biggest jerks in school. When he walked through the crowded Aiken High hallways, the throngs of students seemed to part way in front of him, like Moses crossing the Red Sea. Some people considered Theo to be aloof and arrogant. There was some truth to that. From his six foot seven height he did, literally, look down on just about everyone in the hallway.

Having watched his father start and grow the family business, T.M. Replacement Windows, he knew it took a lot of hard work to be successful. So Theo had adopted a serious, business-like demeanor for himself. He strove for excellence on the football field, in class, and even in how he dealt with other people. His clothes were new and stylish. He was a polished man on his way to do something big.

So it came as a shock to Theo that while working on a lab project in science class, he was summoned to the office of Mrs. Drain. A student had walked into the class and handed Mr.

Peterson a note. Mr. Peterson quickly read the note and scowled. Students who left class during a lab were a disruption to his lesson, and scheduling a make-up lab for the one or two students that seemed to miss every lab wasted his valuable time.

"Mr. Marshall," he called out. "Your presence is requested in Mrs. Drain's office."

Theo had stopped working on the project at the sound of his name and looked up. With the mention of Mrs. Drain, he removed his science safety goggles and raised an eyebrow as if to question Mr. Peterson on whether he had called out the correct name.

"You will have to come back here to Room B317 after school today to complete this lab," said Mr. Peterson.

Theo gathered his notebooks. "But I have to go to practice after school," he complained.

"No," answered Mr. Peterson in his usual condescending tone of voice. "You will come to B317, and finish your work. Athletics preparation can be dealt with on your own personal time."

Theo's usual stoic expression hid his anger. Who wouldn't rather be at practice after school than being stuck in a make-up science lab? He was also a bit worried about going to Mrs. Drain's office, but also kept that to himself. Without another word or crack in his expression, he turned and walked out of B317.

Entering Mrs. Drain's office a little bit of surprise flashed on Theo's face. Drew and Stats were already sitting there, waiting. They were obviously also unhappy to have been pulled out of their classes.

"Oh, damn!" said Stats at the sight of Theo. Both Stats and Drew knew that Theo had never been in any trouble in high school and was proud of it. In a bit of a mocking tone he added, "What now, Mar-shall-not?"

Theo Marshall did not take being made fun of lightly. "Mar-shall-not?" he asked, glaring at Stats. "What the hell does that mean?"

"Nothing,'" said Stats shaking his head dismissively, "since you know nothing.'"

"At least I know enough," retorted Theo angrily, "to be able to graduate high school."

Stung by the insult, Stats stood up, squared his shoulders and pointed his index finger at the larger teenager. Before he could say anything or move closer, Drew jumped up in between them and said, "Guys, hey! Relax, will you? Come on, let's sit down."

It occurred to Drew how little Theo and Stats had in common. Theo was from an upper middle class family, wore new clothes, and acted like he was ready to run a Fortune 500 company. If it weren't for his size and toughness on the foot-ball field, he would probably be considered a stuck-up rich kid. Stats, who lived in the development on the other side of Aiken, came from a single parent family and was certainly not flying to Florida for the winter break. Even though they both played on the football team, they didn't really know each other. They looked at each other through the lens of class stereotypes.

Trying to distract them Drew asked, "Do either of you know what Drain's up to now?"

Theo and Stats both grumbled, "No."

"Probably has to do with that Jeremy kid," said Theo.

"Short bus?" asked Stats using a new nickname for Jeremy.

"Yes," said Theo, not impressed with the joke. "Monique tells me that he's real sick."

Drew was about to blurt out a 'sick in the head' joke but Stats broke in first.

"You?" he asked incredulously. "You were talking to Monique?" It was amazing that he could throw such a big insult with so few words.

"I can talk to whomever I want to," growled Theo leaning across Drew toward Stats.

Once again Drew pushed his body in between the two. "What do you mean by sick?" he asked. "How sick?"

Theo shrugged his shoulders and was about to answer when the door opened and Mrs. Drain marched into the room.

"Mr. Declan. Mr. Timlin. Mr. Marshall," she greeted them coolly. "I'm afraid we have a serious discipline problem with members of the running team."

She paused for a moment to let the threat of discipline sink into the boys. "I'm sure you know that there has been a rash of vandalism across Aiken, and after a thorough investigation I have learned that it was members of the running team who were responsible. Vandalism is a serious offense that we take very seriously, and the perpetrators will have to be punished accordingly."

The three teenagers sat there stone faced. They had no idea what she was talking about.

Drew was relieved she said nothing about his fight with Jeremy. It had been a few days and Jeremy had not shown up at practice. Maybe, he hoped, she hadn't heard about the fight.

"What kind of vandalism, Mrs. Drain?" asked Theo.

"Destruction of public and private property. A gang of boys were observed running through the streets defacing and damaging as they went," answered Mrs. Drain. When she saw that the three still had no idea what she was talking about, she added, "With baseball bats."

Now Drew knew where this was heading, but he was able to keep his face neutral. She must be referring to the "Swing for the Fence" run the distance guys had a few weeks before. They grabbed the baseball team's bats and tapped, rapped, and banged every stop sign and fire hydrant for a five mile loop of Aiken. But the guys never said they broke anything with the bats. Just light taps.

Neither Theo nor Stats still had any idea of what Mrs. Drain was getting at. Theo would have been in the weight room, and Stats, being a sprinter, never left the track.

"Mrs. Drain," said Theo politely pointing out the obvious. "We don't play baseball."

"I know that," snapped Mrs. Drain. "As the tri-captains of the running club," Drew winced at her calling the indoor track team the running club, "I expect you to give me the names of the boys who were involved, or there will be serious consequences."

"You want us to give you names?" asked Stats in his lawyer voice. Theo gave him a quick look. Stats continued, "When exactly did the incident take place? And what, exactly, was damaged?"

Theo joined in, "Can you describe the people in question? What were they wearing?"

Drew was happy to let the other two do all the talking. The less he said, the better.

"I am the one who is asking the questions," said Mrs. Drain, her voice rising. She continued to threaten the three, and demanded the names of the perpetrators. The more she talked, though, it became clear she didn't have much more information. She seemed to be making up the details as she went. Drew figured she was just bluffing to gain a new bargaining chip to use against them.

"How can we tell you who they may have been if we don't have any description of them?" asked Theo.

"You have to know something to drag us out of our classes, you know what I'm saying?" said Stats.

"What other ragtag, mismatched group of boys is running around the city in the dead of winter? It was you," she said, pointing a finger at Drew. "I'm sure of it."

But she didn't really sound so sure.

"Ragtag?" asked Theo, leaning forward.

Stats leaned forward too. "Miss mash?" said Stats, changing up what she had said a bit.

Drew saw his opening. He sat up straight and asked, "You mean they weren't wearing our uniforms?"

Mrs. Drain let silence give her answer. The report she had read said nothing about the gang wearing uniforms.

"Well, then it couldn't possibly be anyone on the indoor team," Drew said with just the slightest hint of a smile. "Because, as you know, Mrs. Drain, we all have brand new, crisp running jackets."

The distance guys had been wearing the relics of Aiken High sports uniform history on the Swing for the Fence run, not their new indoor jackets, but it had become obvious to Drew that Mrs. Drain didn't know that. Now he was the one bluffing.

The three teammates relaxed and sat back in their chairs.

Mrs. Drain's mouth opened, but in what may have been the first time in her school administrative career, no words came out. She had been beaten again. "The investigation will continue," she said weakly.

Mrs. Drain had been trying to use the threat of discipline to get the boy's cooperation. Once again, Jeremy's status as an Aiken High athlete was in jeopardy, and she still needed him to succeed if she wanted to expand the PRISM program. She didn't get to this point in her career by giving up easily. She regrouped, changed her tactics, and began again.

"Boys, you are obviously very smart, and have shown strong leadership to your classmates," she complimented the three. "I'm calling on your maturity and good nature to help support a teammate who has been stricken with a terrible blow."

Theo, Drew and Stats were suspicious.

"Who's that?" asked Stats.

"Your teammate, Jeremy..."

At the mention of Jeremy's name the three guys winced. They each disliked Jeremy for their own reasons. Drew wondered if news of the fight had gotten to Mrs. Drain after all, and he still faced suspension.

".. has been diagnosed with cancer," continued Mrs. Drain, "and will be out of school for a while as he recuperates."

The shock of such a serious illness kept the guys quiet. The self-assured cockiness they felt after calling Mrs. Drain's bluff on the vandalism accusation had quickly drained away.

"Mrs. Drain," Theo spoke up, "What kind of cancer?"

Mrs. Drain hesitated. "I'm afraid that is confidential." She actually had a look of concern and compassion on her face. She was obviously trying to decide what information she could tell them. "In fact, the type of cancer he has is fairly common in young men like yourselves. If diagnosed early it is very treatable, but there is some stigma that prevents some boys from asking for help," she said.

"What stigma?" asked Stats.

"Well," said Mrs. Drain. Finally she made up her mind. For their own good they should know. "Jeremy has testicular cancer. Thankfully he has a good prognosis, and in time, should recover."

Drew was torn. He knew how deadly cancer could be and felt sympathy for anyone with such a serious illness. On the other hand, he still hated the insulting, crude, and bullying Jeremy. Just a few days before he was trying to punch the jerk as hard as he could.

Mrs. Drain thought this was a good teaching moment. "All young men should do a monthly testicular self-exam," she said, holding up her index finger and thumb and rotating them to approximate the self-exam motion, "to become familiar with the shape and size of their testicies..."

"Yo! Stop!" yelled Stats. The awkwardness of Mrs. Drain talking about their testicles was too much for the guys.

Drew thought he would be funny at Jeremy's expense. "You mean he has cancer in his.."

A sharp slap from the back of Theo's hand landed on the side of Drew's face. Pointing his index finger right at Drew's nose, Theo growled, "Hey, there ain't NOTHING funny about cancer."

The right side of Drew's head buzzed with the sting of the slap. A flash of anger quickly faded when he realized that if Theo really wanted to hurt him he would be much worse off. And, more significantly, Theo was right. In a few months he would graduate and never have to see Jeremy again, but someone facing cancer will always have the nagging possibility of relapse in the back of their minds. His face flushed red—with embarrassment.

Theo quickly got hold of his anger. He had just slapped another student right in front of a teacher. He relaxed his muscles, sat up in his chair, and adopted his usual calm face. "You were saying, Mrs. Drain?"

Nothing about this conversation had gone the way Mrs. Drain had expected, and she hadn't even gotten to her point yet. Ignoring the slap, she let out a big sigh and decided to move on. "As teammates and captains of the running team, I expect you to show your support for your teammate. You have one more game this season, and there will be a pep rally so the whole school can show their support for Jeremy," said Mrs. Drain.

"A rally? For Jeremy?" asked Drew.

"A rally? For track?" asked Stats incredulously. Turning to Drew he added. "We never got a football rally. And you get a track rally?"

"That's ridiculous," said Theo ambiguously.

"The event has already been scheduled," said Mrs. Drain emphatically. She was regaining her momentum. "And the three of you, as team captains, will speak at the rally in support of Jeremy."

"Mrs. Drain," said Theo, shaking his head. "I can't do that. I'm not too good at public speaking," he offered lamely.

Mrs. Drain crossed her arms. Looking at Drew she said, "You don't think I heard about your fight in the basement hallway? Fighting can lead to suspension, and removal from team activities," she threatened. Turning to Theo she added, "And you think you can get away with assaulting a student in my office?"

Theo and Drew started to protest, but Mrs. Drain held up her hand to cut them off. "That's it! If you want to finish your senior season on an Aiken High team," she said, finally coming to the point, "You will support your teammate and speak at the school pep rally. Do you understand me?"

After all their swift thinking and bluff calling, Drew and the guys had no more smart answers for Mrs. Drain. There was nothing in this world Drew wanted more than to lead his team to the state indoor meet and bring home a championship. He had done so much work, from recruiting guys, organizing weekend long runs, to practically managing the practices. If he had to do one more thing—one lousy thing—to get the team to the state meet he would do it.

"Say, now," said Stats, shaking his head. "There's no way I'm speaking at any..."

"We'll do it," Drew broke in.

Theo and Stats shot a look at him.

"We'll do it," Drew repeated standing up. "We are going to the state meet, and we are going to win." Turning to his friends he added, "Let's go and figure out what we will say."

As they started to walk out Mrs. Drain, with a slight smile of her own, called after them. "Oh, and a reporter from the Aiken Chronicle will be interviewing you as well."

| 19 |

There hadn't been an undefeated NEMAC championship team from Aiken High since the 1978 baseball team—ancient history. There had been some NEMAC winners, but none of them were lossless. The River Hawks boys indoor team, standing at 6–0 with one final meet to go in the regular season, were poised to be one of the best Aiken teams ever.

The basketball and hockey teams, the popular spectator sports of the winter season that normally grabbed the student body's attention, had losing seasons. Few students bothered to attend their games anymore, and there was a serious void in something for the school to cheer for.

The possibility of an undefeated season had caught the attention of some people in school, mostly guys on the other winter season teams. When Drew walked through the hallways between classes, he heard an occasional, "Good luck" or "Get it done" from a hockey player or wrestler. The words of encouragement always came from a player who knew from experience how lousy it was when your team lost, and how awesome it felt when you won. It was difficult to beat every team in the conference, and the indoor team was getting some respect from guys who knew what an accomplishment it was.

The final meet of the regular season was also a chance to see how the River Hawks measured up against their biggest challenger at the state championship meet, The Seacoast Wave. Being a regional school that pulled kids from the suburban towns along the coast, Seacoast always had large, talented teams that racked up high point totals. Beating them and winning the NEMAC was something the River Hawks hadn't done in years. Drew was convinced the River Hawks had the manpower to run with the Wave and win both meets.

The meet was also the last chance to run a qualifying time and make the A Set. The Loganikos brothers and Tooch were under pressure to reach the qualifying marks. Tooch, especially, seemed tense. In every track workout he hung on Drew's shoulder, trying to match the speed and endurance of his captain and mentor.

The announcement of the mandatory, school wide pep rally was a surprise to the students and teachers. Years ago Aiken High had pep rallies for the football team the day before the Thanksgiving break, but there had never been one during the winter season. Mr. Peterson railed to his students, complaining of the disruption to his lesson plan. Most students were indifferent to the track team, but wouldn't mind spending a period in the bleachers of The Nest rather than in their normal class.

Mrs. Drain had even ensured that the Aiken High Marching Band play at the rally. The band season had ended with the last football game, and by winter most of the musicians had moved on to orchestra. Since there was little time to rehearse, it was decided the band would perform the one song they played the most during the football season.

In August, a longtime member of the school committee and former Aiken High football player died of a heart attack while canoeing with his family in New Hampshire. The only thing Mr. O'Callaghan loved more than Aiken High football was country music, and as a tribute the marching band was forced to learn his favorite song, Elvira, the country-pop hit by the southern gospel vocal quartet, the Oak Ridge Boys. After every touchdown, rather than play the school's fight song, the marching band belted out a lifeless rendition of the ten-year-old country song. By Thanksgiving it was the most universally disliked musical arrangement in the entire school.

With the rally quickly approaching everyone in school now knew who was on the indoor team, and that they had a chance to beat Seacoast. Just about all of the guys on the team started wearing their River Hawks running jackets in the halls between classes. Guys on the football team had always worn team shirts while in school, but runners wearing matching jackets in school? —that was definitely a first.

The notable exception was Asher Dane. He claimed that wearing the River Hawks jackets in school promoted "an unhealthy climate of over competition." Normally the other guys would tease a teammate for saying something out of the ordinary, but they didn't know how to respond to Asher. His ideas were so outside their normal sphere of thought. So they ignored him. On a team that accepted each other whether they were blue collar or white collar, native or immigrant, Christian, Jewish, Muslim, or Buddhist, Asher was being isolated because of his personal philosophy. At practice, lying on his high jump mat he looked as if he were the sole survivor of a shipwreck, floating in a vast sea.

The rest of the guys soaked up their popularity, and for the first time in his high school years, Drew felt that the team—his team—really mattered. His teammates walked the halls with pride, and were motivated to train hard and give it their all. It mattered to the other kids in the school that their school could be the best in the league—at anything—and may be the best in the state. Some of the teachers seemed to be swept up in the excitement. His old Spanish teacher, Ms. Ramirez, wished him well. "Buena suerte con tus carreras, Señor Declan," she said as he passed by in the hall.

"Thanks," answered Drew.

It was the rally posters that sapped all the pride and good feeling out of Drew. In the span of one period there were more rally posters up on the walls of Aiken High than all the anti-drug posters he had seen in the last four years. Throughout the halls, above the water coolers, and on the doors of classrooms were printed posters advertising the mandatory pep rally. Mrs. Drain had arranged for a local car dealership to purchase a large advertisement in the school newspaper, and in exchange, the whole newspaper staff had to make and put up pep rally posters.

In addition to the River Hawks logo and the time and place of the rally, there was the extra bold headline, "Do it for Jeremy." An oversized cut out of Jeremy's face was plastered on each and every poster. The picture was, by far, the most dominant feature of each poster. It was Jeremy, with his tight knit blond hair and his eyes wide open. He had a smile that looked like a normal smile to people who did not know him, but was easily identified by those who did as a twisted sneer.

Drew's stomach was in knots. Everywhere he looked in school—in the cafeteria, above the hallway lockers, even on the door to The Nest—was Jeremy. Seeing Jeremy's picture was bad enough but the sentence, "Do it for Jeremy," made Drew boil. There was even one in Spanish, "Hazlo por Jeremy."

Since Jeremy didn't actually go to Aiken High, very few people knew him. To just about everyone who was not on the indoor team (and the basketball team) Jeremy was just a kid like them who was battling a life-threatening disease. Which was, Drew had to admit, true. But with his picture on every poster, Jeremy had become, literally, the face of the River Hawks indoor team. Not Coach Pilette, not the sprinters, not the shot putters, not distance runners, and most disturbing of all to his ego, not Drew.

Between periods kids in the halls asked Drew about Jeremy's health, hoping to hear some news of his recovery. One fresh-man, on the verge of tears, asked for reassurance, "He's going to be all right, isn't he?"

Repeating back what Mrs. Drain had said, Drew answered in an emotionless voice, "He has a good prognosis, and in time, should recover."

He wanted to tell them what a jerk Jeremy was. How he bul-lied JB. His insulting and racist comments. But how can you bad mouth someone fighting cancer and has his face on every poster in the school? You can't. He resolved to ride out the Jeremy wave with his best teenage indifference. It was just one more thing he had to get through to make sure the River Hawks won.

In Mr. Peterson's science lab, Drew endured Shelley and Linda's ruminations on Jeremy.

"He's got to be in a good hospital," said Shelley. "What's the survival rate for this?"

"They're good," said Lynda, answering one of the questions. "I guess he is too sick to come to the rally, right? I think it is a specialized one."

"All hospitals are specialized, or maybe they have departments that are specialized," said Shelley. "Think his room has a view?"

"Of the rally? Doubt it." said Linda with a laugh. Turning to Drew as if he had just entered the room Linda asked, "So, how is he doing?"

Drew drew in a breath and deadpanned, "He has a good prognosis, and in time, should recover."

At the rally Mrs. Drain was back to her smiling, confident self. Her goal of expanding the PRISM program and getting her kids the education they deserved hinged on getting more students into Aiken High. That Jeremy didn't mesh with the other boys on the team had not deterred her a bit. Using the dual marketing tools of the posters and the rally she had gotten her student into the hearts and minds of the main student population. Surely, many of the students would go home and tell their parents of Jeremy's rally and soon the idea of PRISM students in Aiken High would seem commonplace.

"Now, team captain Andrew Declan will say a few words about Jeremy's contribution to the team," Mrs. Drain announced to the capacity crowd in The Nest.

Drew leaned an elbow on the lectern, and in an exasperated voice began, "Jeremy has..." There was a long awkward pause as Drew tried to get some positive words out of his mouth. He looked up at the ceiling as if searching for inspiration. "... a good prognosis," he continued, falling back on his rehearsed line, "and in time, should recover."

Sitting with the rest of the indoor team Casey started a one person applause. The rest of the team joined in, and slowly the whole audience gave a polite, unenergetic applause.

"Thank you," concluded Drew. He slouched his shoulders and walked back to his seat as the marching band started their final, cheerless performance of Elvira.

After the rally it was a relief to get to the locker room with his teammates. They had about an hour to kill before the Seacoast teams arrived for the meet. It was time they used to speak freely about how much they disliked Jeremy, even while still acknowledging that they wouldn't wish cancer on anyone. They were all glad he was not around anymore; it was just too bad that it was something so serious that made it happen. More than anything they felt that their team's identity had been hijacked and they were looking to take it back.

It was Casey who broke the tension and got the guys laughing with a perfectly timed "Swing for the Fence" joke.

When the laughter died down Drew asked, "Whatever happened to the bats?" Even though Mrs. Drain seemed to be mollified with the student rally, Drew wanted to make sure no one got in trouble for the alleged vandalism during the Swing for the Fence run.

"At first, we stashed them behind Tooch's restaurant," said Gil.

"After about five miles those things got heavy," added Casey helpfully.

"Guys, they belong to the baseball team," reprimanded Drew. "You have to return them."

"Relax," said Casey. "We got them yesterday." He had borrowed his stepmom's car and with Gill and Tooch drove to the restaurant and retrieved them.

"We'll put them back in the equipment room the next time the coast is clear," assured Gil.

The River Hawks were fired up for the last meet of the season. There were actually some spectators standing beyond the far turn of The Nest. Gil and Casey never had friends watch them before, and they were determined to make a good showing by getting the top two spots in their race. Making the A Set was all that Tooch could think of, and he was intent on running a qualifying time. Avenging their humiliating loss to the Seacoast Wave last fall and being NEMAC champions gave an extra push to the football players. Drew was ready to reclaim his role as the anchor of the River Hawks. He was going to throw all of his frustration of the last week into running a dominant performance.

Under the technical eye of Coach Pillette, Drew was in the best fitness of his life. He still maintained his strength from all the long runs of the fall and early winter, and now his interval training had sharpened his speed. He had been hitting fast splits in training and there had been moments when it felt so easy. There was a burning desire in Drew to know just how fast he could run a mile. How long could he hold the pace and still press for more? What was the limit his body could endure? This would be the day he would find out.

In the final minutes before the call for the mile, Drew looked around to size up his competitors. Having gone over the coaches' reports with Stats a thousand times he knew that Seacoast had a miler with some impressive times, and he wanted to put a face to the name. He wasn't concerned with losing, he just wanted to keep an eye on any runner who might challenge him.

As Drew approached the starting line he noticed something familiar about Seacoast's best miler. It was a combination of the kid's curly red hair, how his shoulders were a bit rolled over, and how his elbows angled out from his waist. Drew knew he had raced the guy before, but where?

"Hey, we need those five points from you," said Stats. Unlike basketball or hockey games where a scoreboard continuously displayed the team totals, track officials kept the running tallies to themselves on their clipboards. It was up to someone on each team to keep track of the score and spread the word to the rest of the runners. Stats kept a running total of the team points in his head and was reporting to Drew what the River Hawks needed to keep ahead of Seacoast. Drew nodded. He assumed that the team needed him to win the mile and earn the five points.

Turning to Tooch, Stats added, "This meet is clooooose, know what I'm saying? Little Tooch-man, you have to come up big and grab us a point." Tooch, who was shaking out each leg to stay loose, shook his head nervously.

The starter called the milers onto the track and lined them up. Drew, being the number one runner of the home team, was assigned the inside of lane one. Looking sideways at Seacoast's number one runner, it dawned on Drew. This guy was Runner Ten from the state cross country race. The runner that had gone out too fast, tried to hang on to Drew in the final stretch, but wilted in the final ten yards.

Noticing that Drew was staring at him, Runner Ten scoffed, "What are you looking at?"

Drew knew there was no way he was going to let this guy beat him in the mile, at his home track, in the final home meet of his senior year. He narrowed his eyes and said, "I am going to run you into the ground."

Before Runner Ten had a chance to respond the starter announced, "Take your mark!" and all of the milers moved up to the starting line. Drew looked straight down the track and focused his attention on unleashing his energy into the race.

The starter squeezed the trigger on the gun, and a sharp crack echoed off the walls of The Nest. The runners burst forward, jostling for position. The top runners wanted to get as close to the pole as possible entering the first turn. Coach Pilette taught them how important it was to establish position on the inside. If a runner was caught in an outside lane, over the course of a mile they would run another five yards compared to the runners on the line. In a tight race that came down to the wire, those few extra yards could make the difference.

Drew just about sprinted to the top of the turn and gained his position. After the interval competition with Jeremy, he vowed to never let any other runner get the inside again. Runner Ten and the others folded in behind Drew for the first turn.

Normally, once he had established his lead position Drew would slow down to his normal mile race pace. Not today. Not in his final home race of his senior year. Not after all the signs that said, "Do it for Jeremy." This wasn't Jeremy's team. It was his team. This was his track. He was going to show everyone that he was the captain. That he was the heart and soul of the team. That he was the best athlete in the school, and with him leading the way the River Hawks were going to win the state championship.

Coach Pilette instantly saw Drew's pace was faster than it should be. So many runners, usually the inexperienced ones, go out too fast and fade in the final stretch. The pack of runners quickly stretched out, single file behind Drew. Only two runners, Runner Ten and Tooch made any attempt to keep up. Coach ran across the infield just in time to hear the quarter mile split. "Sixty-three, sixty-four, sixty-five..."

"Slow down!" shouted Coach Pilette. There was no way, he felt, that Drew could hold a 63-second 440 pace for the rest of the race.

Drew held the pace. Runner Ten decided to meet the challenge and moved up to Drew's outside shoulder. Both runners leaned into the curves, their arms and legs temporarily in sync.

The rest of the River Hawks had never heard Coach Pilette yell that loud, and certainly not at Drew. Since when does a coach yell at his top runner to slow down? As Coach Pilette ran across the infield to get to the half mile split, a group of kids from both the boys and girls team followed.

On the back straightaway Runner Ten made his move, pulling up shoulder to shoulder with Drew. For about fifteen yards the two runners flew down the track side by side just a few inches separating them. Drew drifted slightly out from the inside, not enough to block Runner Ten, but enough to make Runner Ten run wider. At the top of the turn Drew sharply leaned back into the turn and cut tight to the line. Runner Ten tried to match the move but he was now about two-and-a-half feet behind Drew on the curve.

"Two-o-nine, two-ten.." called out the timer at the half mile. "

"Save some for the last lap!" yelled Coach Pilette, still afraid Drew would blow up and get passed by the rest of the pack.

The Seacoast head coach had the same fear. If his guy continued at this pace he might not even finish. He needed his runners to score points. "Take it easy! Take it easy!" he implored.

"What's he doing?" asked Casey as a group of guys gathered to watch the runners pass. "A 2:09 half? That's crazy."

Gil grabbed Stats by the arm. "Stats, what's the school record for the mile?"

At first Stats was offended that Gil had grabbed him, but the power of the question took over his emotions. "Four nineteen point two. Some Irish dude named Mc-something in 1968."

"That's it!" shouted Gil. "Drew's going for the school record!"

Heading toward the three quarter split, Runner Ten began to lose ground on Drew. If he had a good kick on the last lap he could still be in contention, but the gap between them became wider.

The two coaches waved their arms, trying to get the attention of their number one milers. They wanted their guys to run a more tactical race. "Slow down!" yelled the Seacoast coach.

A girl's voice broke through the coaches' shouts. "Go Drew! Break the record!" shouted Mary.

"Who's number one?" shouted Stats. "You're number one!"

The rest of the River Hawks joined in yelling and screaming encouragement to their captain.

"Three-fifteen, three-sixteen..." read out the timer at the ¾ split.

Over the shouts of the team Gil said, "He's got to run under sixty-five for the last quarter."

"Oh man," said Casey. "I think he's slowing down."

Stats was disgusted with the negativity. "Hey 'y'all," he said. "You have Drew Declan out there. Records are going to fall today, you know what I'm saying?"

The gap between Drew and Runner Ten widened. The Seacoast runner's head was tilted back swaying side to side. His elbows wobbled out far from his chest. His stride shortened. The Seacoast coach put his hands on his head in exasperation. Runner Ten was falling back, and moving up strongly behind him was Tooch.

The River Hawks ran across the infield in mass and lined up along the far straightaway. Drew had a lap and a half to go, and he knew he couldn't afford to slow down. When it came to mile splits, he could do the math in his head as well as Stats. He had to run sub sixty-five over the last quarter, and it was going to hurt. Chin down, with his arms in perfect form, Drew opened up his stride and did what he was put here on earth to do: run faster.

The team was now on both the infield and on the outside side of the track, forming a human tunnel that Drew sliced through. Teammates were jumping, and cheering, and yelling and screaming. The sound was riotous, bouncing off the walls and ceiling of The Nest. Coach Pilette, caught up in the excitement, changed his attitude. "Dig deep! Dig deep!" he cheered.

The pain in Drew's gut grew. His legs felt as if they were weighted down with a wet pair of jeans. His lungs filled and expelled with every stride. He was all alone in the lead for the race. There was no one to help with the pace or push him. It was just him, in control of his body, churning closer and closer to being the fastest miler to ever walk the halls of Aiken High School. Here on his home turf, with its crazy 200 yard track, he had to lay it on the line for the last ¾ lap.

With one more burst of motivation, Drew unleashed his kick. How many times had he surprised his opponents over the last ¾ lap to win? Today he unleashed his kick against the biggest opponent of all: his own body.

Behind him Runner Ten was flailing. His stride had shortened, his shoulders and arms were tense and rigid. His whole upper body was clenched and his chin pointed up toward the ceiling. Turning his head to see if anyone was coming up behind him his eyes went wide. Tooch was bearing down on him.

Finally over his cold, and without any nagging injuries, Tooch was running the strongest race of his life. He had gone out faster than Coach Pilette wanted, but the excitement of Drew's speed had sucked him in. To his own surprise the pace had not sapped his strength, and with a lap to go he had plenty left to finish strong. With Runner Ten sputtering ahead of him, Tooch focused on claiming second place for himself.

In the last few yards of his race Drew started to tighten up a little bit. He had perfectly measured out his strength for the race, leaving nothing left in his tank as he leaned forward, chest out, and crossed the finish line at The Nest for the last time.

It took two or three strides for him to come to a halt. The instant relief from pain felt wonderful. His chest was heaving, breaths filling and emptying his lungs. He became a bit dizzy as the blood rushed away from his head to his extremities. He put his hands on his knees to maintain balance, and let the pain drain from his lungs and legs. Saliva filled his mouth, his cheeks felt puffy, and for a moment he thought he might throw up.

Teammates ran up and surrounded Drew, patting him on the back. With his balance becoming more stable, he stood up straight, and gave out high fives.

Coach Pilette cut through the crowd holding out his stopwatch for Drew to see. The large black numbers on the gray background read 4:18.85. With a wide smile Coach Pilette said, "You are the fastest River Hawk miler, ever."

Runner Ten gave one last push to hold off Tooch, but it only lasted a few strides. Tooch, chin down, arms pumping, powered into second place. There was no doubt that he had run a qualifying time, and when he crossed the finish line he threw his arms in the air like an Olympic champion. It was the breakthrough race he had been waiting for, and he jumped in the air to celebrate.

Stumbling toward the finish line at barely a jog, Runner Ten was passed by a freshman River Hawk named Harlin, and another Seacoast runner. He fell to the track after the finish line, defeated, spent, and demoralized.

"Hey, you!" called Stats trying to get Drew's attention. "We just swept the mile. There's no way they're beating us now.

We've got the points." Even with the relay race to come and the final score of the field events incomplete, Stats knew, with mathematical certainty, that the River Hawks were NEMAC champions. With a sly smile he added, "Do. You. Know..."

The other guys joined in and the teammates finished the phrase together, "What. I'm! Saying!"

The mile finish electrified the River Hawks. Gone was the somber and melancholy feeling that came from the forced pep rally. The River Hawks were euphoric with the victory over their toughest rival. They were confident, and ready to prove to the whole state what they believed to be true: they were the best.

With a 4:18 mile under his belt, Drew would be considered a top contender in the state meet. But he still desired that larger goal: to lead his team over the finish line and win the state championship. Looking around at the guys who were his team-mates—his River Hawks—Drew couldn't wait for the final and most important meet of the season.

The mood in the locker room was celebratory. Guys were recounting stories of their races and pumping each other up for the next challenge. Tooch was beaming with all the praise and congratulations he got from his teammates. His qualifying time had cemented him in the A Set, and his pride made him seem three inches taller than he was before the day's race. Theo joked that he was going to put Tooch up on his shoulders and run a victory lap.

The good time was interrupted by an ear splitting crash of aluminum on aluminum. The bang bounced off the walls of the locker room and silenced the guys. A second bang rang out from the back of the locker room.

The aluminum sound was partly familiar. It had to be one of the bats from the Swing for the Fence run. Mark Loganikos, with his fists tightly clenched on a bat loomed over a trash barrel. A fierce angry scowl on his face, he raised his large arms over his head and swung down. With each powerful blow the barrel became more deformed and disfigured.

Mark failed to throw a qualifying distance in the meet. No one gets cut from track, but they can be left behind. His twin, Michael had qualified. One brother would go on, one would stay home. The barrel, now shaped more like a question mark than a cylinder, was the target of Mark's anger, disappointment, and sadness.

With one last crushing blow, Mark tossed the bat aside. Tears brimming in his eyes, he walked silently out of the locker room and toward the showers.

The team was stunned into silence. They all knew the feeling of disappointment, and could sympathize with Mark. At one point in the past they had all failed to make a team. For a moment their good mood was put on hold.

Drew grabbed Casey by the shoulders. "Get those bats out of here and back to the baseball storage room," he commanded.

The damaged barrel could get the team in trouble. It seemed that there was always one potential disaster that could derail the team's chances. Drew grabbed Tooch. "The school is just about empty this time of day," he started. "Take this barrel up to room B317," he said referring to Mr. Peterson's science lab, "And swap it out with that one."

"Don't you think Mr. Peterson will notice?" asked Theo skeptically.

"Sure," answered Drew, "But he'll never think the track team did it. We don't have bats in our locker room." With a confident smile he added, "Nothing is going to stop us from being state champions."

No team from Aiken High had come close to winning a state championship in years. Last winter, boys basketball went into the post-season playoffs with a team stocked with seniors, but were eliminated in the first round. This season their team started mostly underclassmen, and compiled a dismal record. Their trainer and number one fan, JB, was the sole student who believed they had a chance to make the playoffs.

The only posters in the school hallways were the ones for the indoor team. They hadn't been made by true fans and had Jeremy's face on them, yet they had their desired effect. Students in Aiken High knew that the boys indoor team had a real chance to be champions.

The pep rally, despite its mandatory attendance requirement, also seemed to build some excitement throughout the school. When word got around that the River Hawks beat Seacoast, and Drew broke the school record, there was an indisputable authentic buzz about the team.

Guys on the team moved through school with something that members of a track team had never experienced before: recognition. People knew who they were, what distances they ran, and if they had qualified for the River Hawks state meet team. It was the kind of pride that Theo and Stats, who had been on the football team all four years, only dreamed about. For the previously unknown and unheralded runners, it was thrilling.

A few hockey and basketball players were jealous. They played on the real sports teams, and even with losing records felt they deserved more respect than runners. But the person in Aiken High who was the most jealous was The Deuce.

The man's loyalty to the River Hawks was unquestionable. He was an assistant football coach, attended every wrestling match and basketball game, and had even procured the new equipment for the inaugural season of lacrosse. In one way or another, The Deuce had been part of every big moment in Aiken High School sports since his own years playing on the football team.

It was killing him that he had absolutely nothing to do with this year's boys indoor track team. He had not been to a single meet. The new coach, Pilette, had never asked him for advice. Even the new uniforms were purchased through a different budget than his.

Most of all, The Deuce was taken by surprise. In all his years he had never seen the school rally for a team like this—especially a track team. There was probably some support for the team because of the Lamonda kid's illness, he thought. Who wouldn't support a kid with cancer? But no one in the school knew the kid, and it didn't seem like anyone on the track team liked him. When the kid recovers and comes back to school, he would still have to make sure the guys on the basketball team didn't kill him.

It all seemed to lead back to Declan, thought The Deuce. The kid managed to get his team new uniforms. Somehow he got a school wide pep rally for—for god's sake—the track team. And even though he disliked and fought with the sick boy, he used the sympathy angle and put Jeremy's face on all those posters. Obviously, The Deuce concluded, Declan was ruthless. The kid would stop at nothing to promote his team.

"Why are you here?" The Deuce confronted Drew as he entered the main locker room. He sounded grouchy. "How come you didn't get suspended for that fist fight?" Although he hadn't reported the fight, he assumed other teachers had heard about it.

"Ah, I don't..." sputtered Drew.

"Who's idea was it to have a rally?" The Deuce asked, poking a finger at Drew. "Yours?"

"No," said Drew, proclaiming his innocence. "It wasn't my.."

The Deuce wasn't buying Drew's denials. He was convinced that Drew was at the center of all of it. "Do it for Jeremy?" The Deuce asked skeptically. "How'd you come up with that one?"

Drew's face fell. His eyes narrowed. "I had nothing to do with that," he said firmly.

Over the years, The Deuce dealt with all kinds of kids and had learned how to read teenagers. No one could lie to The Deuce and get away with it. This last answer, he concluded, was true. He had clearly hit a nerve with Declan, and decided to lighten up.

"Well, it's a good thing—cheering for a sick teammate," said The Deuce.

Drew gave no reply.

"And with all this excitement you've built up here," said The Deuce with a smile creeping on his face, "you better not lose."

"We're going to win," said Drew confidently.

The Deuce turned to end the conversation, but then a thought came to him. It probably had nothing to do with Declan, but it seemed like every other crazy thing around here did. He turned back to Drew and bluffed. "Oh, I want my bat back." The Deuce had recently done an inventory for the upcoming baseball season and one aluminum baseball bat was missing.

"What bats?" said Drew, his expression showing a bit of false denial. "I don't know where the bats are. Have you checked the equipment locker?"

"Of course I checked the equipment locker!" roared The Deuce. His hunch was right. He liked this kid, but no one was going to get away with stealing his equipment. "I want that bat back or you won't be on that bus Friday night."

"Ok," said Drew meekly. "If I hear anything about it I'll let you know. I promise."

"I want it back before Friday," demanded The Deuce. Then dismissing Drew he said, "Now get out of here and go run."

Coach Ethan Pilette was having an exciting winter. In his first coaching job, his River Hawks were undefeated and the winners of the NEMAC league. Some may dismiss this accomplishment by saying that he inherited a strong team with a core group of runners, but the times don't lie. His runners had significantly improved throughout the season. Even the basketball dropout who had joined the team midseason had run some impressive times. Most of all he had perfectly tailored the season's workouts so the runners were peaking just in time for the state meet.

He had several athletes who had a legitimate shot at winning their events. The sprinter, Timlin, came into the season with raw speed, but an atrocious start. For the indoor 50, a good start was vital to winning at the state level. Early in the season Timlin didn't seem very motivated, but around the time his cousin Keith left the team, the boy became focused on improving. He was very coachable, took corrections and incorporated them into his races.

The shot putter, Marshall, was also a contender at the states. The tall, powerful athlete had concentrated on his technique and made great strides this season. In an honest moment Pilette, who had never seen the inside of The Nest's weight room, would admit that he had little to do with Theo's success. But in the eyes of the outside world, the head coach gets credit when one of his athletes succeeds, and Coach Pilette wasn't going to stop anyone from giving him praise.

The miler, Declan, was the star performer. He had come off a strong cross country season and continued to improve. Pilette had dialed in his training so well that the senior had broken the school record, and was one of the favorites at the states.

The videotape sessions with the high jumper, Dane, had worked, and he was developing the perfect blend of technique and lift. If he could put it all together in one jump, he'd be equal to the top jumpers.

The River Hawks never had so many athletes with qualifying times, and they had the potential to score a lot of points. There were coaches who spent years of their careers without winning a championship, and the possibility of doing it in his first year thrilled Coach Pilette.

If this all weren't exciting enough, Pilette and his wife were expecting their first child, and the due date was coming up. On the side of his skinny hip he wore a pager, the latest communication technology. Whether he was at The Nest, or out on a run, his wife could page him at any time, and let him know if she were starting to go into labor. He wasn't going to miss his baby's birth, even if he had to run to the hospital.

Coach Pilette had Drew gather the team around him before the day's practice. "We are looking, ah, pretty good, I think," he started, "we've got one more speed workout to get you sharp." His delivery had improved little throughout the season, but with only the A Set in attendance, he seemed a little more sure of himself. "After that, uh, we will taper into, uh, Friday's meet."

The team milled around quietly waiting to hear if there was any new information that they didn't already know.

"When we get there, ah well, it's kind of a crazy, big place," he continued. "You can kind of get lost there. So I want you guys to stay together." Normally a track team spreads out in a gym. The sprinters gathered near the starting blocks, the throwers near the cage, and the distance guys often left the gym to warm up in the streets. "And it can be overwhelming. I know you guys are excited, but I don't want you jumping around all crazy. You should be businesslike. Focused. Stay in control."

It occurred to the guys that this was the coach's pre-race speech. It wasn't very motivating, but they had to admit it was the best one he had given all season. Most coaches would have saved the big speech for the day of the meet. Coach Pilette gave his early, and made it as exciting as a textbook.

The workout was short but fast. Coach Pilette wanted to make sure everyone was at full strength for Friday night's meet. The quick intervals they ran were designed to sharpen everyone's speed, and it had the added benefit of making the runners feel fast. As they whipped through the 220s they became more and more confident.

On Friday afternoon the River Hawks would board a bus to the state's Oaks Burdell Track and Community Center, named after a Major League Baseball player who died early in his career. It was odd to see a statue of Oaks, high up on a pedestal, taking a swing with his bronze bat while walking into an indoor running track. To Drew, it was the ultimate insult to his sport that a baseball player, not a runner, was memorialized at the state's biggest running venue. They couldn't find one runner to name the track after? He had nothing against Oaks personally, it was just that baseball was so boring—all that standing around and spitting. But Oaks had been famous and passed away just a few years before construction began on the facility, so teams from across the state would finish their season at "The Oaks."

The track inside The Oaks was a thing of beauty. The rubberized surface was springy underfoot, and every footfall seemed to return energy back to the runner, bouncing them further down the track. The two curves were banked, so that the far outside lane was a yard higher than the inside one. Runners in the faster sprints could fight the centrifugal force of the curve by leaning lower into the turns.

On the wall beyond the far curve was a list of every championship track team since the building was built in the early 1980s. Each year a new team would be forever immortalized when their city, nickname, and logo were etched onto a silver plaque and hung next to the names of all previous champions. There they would remain, a permanent testament to a team that no others could catch.

For Drew Declan, this had been his goal for four years of high school. Even though he was in the best shape of his life and had just broken the school mile record, he knew it was unlikely that he would ever be an individual champion. There were two or three guys in the state who had posted faster times this season. It would take a team effort to win a championship. The collective effort of guys who were fast, guys with stamina, and even strong powerful guys who couldn't run a step, would make the difference. There had always been talented athletes across his school, and this year he had harnessed their efforts and kept them focused on the ultimate goal. There was no doubt in his mind that they would be champions.

| 21 |

"Vandalism is a crime," announced Mr. Peterson as he paced back and forth in front of his class. "Whoever came here into room B317 and defaced school property has shown, not just immaturity," he paused to let the next words sink in, "but criminality!"

The students in class sat expressionless. All but one of them had no idea what Mr. Peterson was talking about. Drew could feel his heart rate increase as he tried to maintain the same neutral expression of his classmates. He was pretty sure that Mr. Peterson wouldn't figure out how his barrel got destroyed, but there was always a risk.

Reaching behind his desk Mr. Peterson held up the crumpled remnants of a trash barrel. "For some people, this is just a trash barrel," he lectured. "But for us here at Aiken High, it is required waste disposal equipment!" Shaking the barrel for all to see, he asked, "How can we perform science without the proper equipment?"

Most of the class was willing to be silent and just wait out Mr. Peterson's tirade. He would probably calm down for the second half of the lab. Monique thought she would have some fun.

"Mr. Peterson, what happened to your barrel? It's all crumpled," she said.

"Obviously someone came in here," he answered while still holding the barrel, "and struck it with blows."

"That would have been loud," said Shelley. She and Linda still shared a lab table with Drew and Monique.

"Like the cans they play in the Caribbean," added Linda.

"Cans? I thought they were barrels," said Shelley. "I'd cover my ears."

"It's very musical," said Linda. "They can play all sorts of songs."

"What is the difference between a can and a barrel, anyways? Is one more scientific?" asked Shelley.

Monique broke in to get some clarity, "Are you girls talking about steel drums?"

At the exact same time Shelley said "No." while Linda said "Yes."

Then they simultaneously questioned each other's answer. "Yes?" asked Shelley while Linda asked, "No?"

After weeks of listening to their incessant drivel, Drew had been cured of his crushes on the twins. Not only that, their race times had plateaued and weren't that impressive. It was Mary McKinnon that was running well, and now had Drew's attention.

"Ladies, please," said Mr. Peterson, regaining control over the conversation. "Does anyone have any information on who came in here and vandalized the equipment?" Mr. Peterson brought his gaze down to Drew. He slowly walked forward to the lab table with the battered barrel held out. "Mr. Declan," he said sternly. "Did you have anything to do with this barrel being damaged here in room B317?"

Drew relaxed. This was going to be easy. The barrel was bashed up in the locker room, not here in B317. "No." he said emphatically.

"You know," pressed Mr. Peterson with a veiled threat, "Anyone involved in school vandalism would be barred from their team and not allowed to play in games."

"I don't play in games, Mr. Peterson," Drew said firmly. "I run in track meets."

Mr. Peterson's demeanor waffled, his interrogation had lost the initiative. He must have believed Drew, for after a few more general threats to the class, he returned to their normal school work. Monique, on the other hand, could tell there was something sly with Drew's answer.

"You really had nothing to do with that barrel at all?" she asked him as they walked in the hall after class.

"Not really," answered Drew with a shrug. "I never touched the thing."

Monique didn't press the issue. She didn't want to know the details, or get involved. She decided to change the topic. "Hey, why is the boy's team taking their own bus Friday night? We could all fit in one bus for this meet?"

It had been his idea to get the boys indoor team its own bus. With their own bus the guys could stay focused and get ready for the meet.

"We just wanted to be together, and get pumped up," said Drew. "Besides, the bus was available."

Since Jeremy illness he hadn't been driven to Aiken High and the short bus he had come on was free. Drew had expected Mrs. Drain to reject the idea, but she immediately made sure it would happen.

"Why?" Drew asked with a smile. "Are you going to miss sitting next to Theo?"

"Shut your mouth!" said Monique with a sheepish grin.

Drew thought he would make her more uncomfortable. "Or sitting next to Stats?"

"Ahh!" she yelled. "Shut your mouth again." She wound up a fist to give Drew a punch on the shoulder, but stopped halfway. Her eyes looked past Drew and her expression became serious. "They're gone." she said.

Drew turned around to see what she had been looking at. Nothing seemed unusual. The lockers lined the walls. The doors to the classrooms were open between periods as usual. The notices on the poster boards were. . . The posters!

Drew looked up and down the halls and there was not one "Do it for Jeremy" track poster. Just before science class the posters had been on the walls, over the lockers and on every door. In just one period they had all vanished.

"The meet is tomorrow," said Drew. He had expected the posters to be up until the day of the championship meet. Normally it took weeks for the janitorial staff to remove outdated posters. There were still some posters advertising a Valentines Day cookie sale, but all the Jeremy posters were gone.

The other students in the hall passed by them oblivious to the change. Monique and Drew stood for a moment, trying to figure out why and how the posters had vanished when a girl approached them.

"Congratulations on your record, Drew," said Mary McKinnon. "What an awesome run."

The look of stupor gave way to a smile on Drew's face. "Aw, thanks," he said. "Hey, you had another good race too. You qualified for states, right?"

"Yeah," said Mary brightly. "I can't wait. My first time at The Oaks."

Monique sighed. "Not too sure about that boys-only bus now, are you, lover boy." She headed off to class leaving Drew and Mary.

"What's that about the bus?" asked Mary.

"Ah, nothing," said Drew, trying to dismiss what Monique was hinting at. "We just noticed all the track posters are gone. All of them! In just one period!"

"Oh," said Mary sadly. "Well they did have Lamonda's face on all of them. They couldn't really have pictures of him up in a school, of course."

"Did he die?" asked Drew with shock. For the first time he honestly felt bad for Jeremy. It truly was a horrible thing when a person dies so young.

"No, no," said Mary. "He's out of the hospital. He's been fine."

It seemed doubtful that someone who just had cancer could be "fine," but Drew wasn't going to argue with her. "Then what?" he asked.

Mary shrugged her shoulders. It was obvious she knew more information but didn't want to say. The hallway started emptying as kids made their way into the classrooms.

Drew prodded, "You can tell me. What is it?"

Mary relented, "All right, but you can't tell anyone. If dad finds out I told you anything, I swear, I'll be grounded till spring."

"Promise," said Drew.

"It's not good," she said, lowering her voice. "He got arrested for selling cocaine within 100 yards of an elementary school again."

Drew was shocked, "What the hell!" But the shock didn't last and incredulous disbelief took hold. "But he was sick," objected Drew. He realized that his first thought was not whether or not Jeremy had the moral deficiency of a drug dealer, but how he could make the transactions if he was so ill. Finally his thoughts turned to Jeremy's athletic ability. The kid had the potential to be one of the best runners in the state, but now he would never compete in a high school again. "What a waste," he finished.

Mary shrugged as if to say it was unfortunate that some people do the wrong thing.

"Are you sure?" asked Drew. There were often a lot of rumors flying around Aiken High, and he didn't want to be fooled into believing something that wasn't true.

Mary shrugged again as if to say of course it was true—why would you doubt her?

Drew felt a wave of attraction to Mary. She had said more with two shrugs of her shoulders than her sisters could spit out in a thousand words. Every time he talked to Mary he felt as if they really connected. Their minds seemed to work in the same way.

"I bet Mrs. Drain had the posters taken down," said Mary.

She was right, Drew thought. Mrs. Drain couldn't have the poster boy of her PRISM program be a drug dealer. That would ruin the chances of other PRISM students of ever being enrolled at Aiken High. The Jeremy experiment was over. He would never be back. The way the halls had been suddenly scrubbed clean of Jeremy's face made it feel as if the kid had never existed.

Drew had grown to respect Mrs. Drain. She was smart, tough, and worked hard for what she thought was important. She would come back next year and find a way to get the PRISM kids a better education.

"Dad always says," said Mary, "crime doesn't pay."

Drew shrugged. "My dad is an engineer, and he says that too."

They laughed as the bell rang for the next period. Mary turned to get to her class and said, "You stay clear of trouble. You don't want to miss the meet."

What trouble could there be left, he wondered. He had thought of everything that could go wrong, and fixed it. It seemed like things were lining up perfectly for the River Hawks tomorrow. But something about Mary's last line made him worry. He had a nagging feeling that there was still one stone unturned. One missing piece to the puzzle.

It hit him with a thunderclap. The missing baseball bat. The one Mark Loganikos used to crush the barrel was still in the locker room. Even though Drew hadn't been on the Swing for the Fence run, The Deuce fingered him to get the punishment if the last bat wasn't returned, and he had to run in the meet if they had any chance to win. It was just one more detail that Drew had to take care of to make sure the River Hawks could take a run at the best teams in the state.

In the empty hallway he stopped short before entering his history class. He had to search the locker room and find the bat right now. If he got reported for skipping class, it would take a few days for the detention slip to come through. By then, he thought, the River Hawks would be state champions.

| **22** |

Students are not allowed to walk around the school during class periods without a hall pass. In the early 1980s, when Drew's older brother and sister were students, there was an "open campus" where students could come and go as they pleased throughout the day. That policy was changed when the administration realized that many of the students who went to Burger King for lunch never came back for afternoon classes.

Now the flow of students was severely limited. During class periods, teachers sat at strategic hallway intersections to stop any student who lingered after the bell rang. There were some legitimate reasons for a student to be in the halls, like going to the nurse's office, meeting with a guidance counselor, or delivering school supplies to a classroom. Even in these cases, the student would have to produce a hall pass. Without one, a student could be written up, sent to the main office, and receive detention.

Drew knew he had some detention coming to him for skipping class, but he didn't want to compound his problem by being caught in the hallway. More importantly, if he was stopped by a hall monitor he could be marched to the main office, and lose his chance to find the missing bat.

On the first floor of the old Aiken High building he peaked around a corner to see if it was clear. Sure enough, there was a teacher sitting in front of the doors to the back staircase. To get to the locker rooms he would have to go down these stairs to the basement and take the tunnel to The Nest. There was never a monitor in the tunnel, so once he made it down the stairs he would be free.

To get around the hall monitor, he would have to take the school's main staircase up to the second floor, then walk down the hallway to the back staircase. Hopefully there wouldn't be a monitor up there. It was a straightforward plan except he had to walk past the administration office to get to the main staircase.

The office windows stretched the entire width of the room, and gave the secretaries a clear view of the hallway. Anyone arriving late to school, or in this case, in between periods, would have to walk by them and be noticed.

Walking quickly, being careful not to linger in front of any of the classroom doors, Drew made his way to the front of the school. He stopped a few yards before the main office windows and got down on all fours. For a moment he considered crawling on the floor beneath the office windows like an Army recruit in basic training, but he discounted the idea. That would take too long and increase the risk of getting caught. And if he was going to get caught he'd rather be standing than crawling on the high school floor.

Quietly Drew whispered, "Runners, to your mark." He placed his hands carefully on the floor in front of him shoulder width apart. "Set," he said, raising himself up in the sprinter's starting position. "Go!"

Drew had watched Stats practice his starts all season long, so he knew what he had to do. Driving his legs and pumping his arms he came to full height and speed just as he came into view of the office windows. Looking forward and sprinting at his top speed he flew past the windows in under two tenths of a second.

The secretaries saw something out of the corner of their eyes, but by the time they looked up from their desks Drew had passed and was seven steps up the staircase.

Working his way down the second floor hall he peeked around the corner to get a view of the door to the back stairs. To his relief, the monitor chair was empty.

Straightening up and getting his breathing under control, he nonchalantly strolled down the hall toward the back stairs. Opening up the door at the top of the staircase he came to a screeching halt. On the top step was his sophomore year Spanish teacher, Mrs. Ramirez.

"Buenas tardes señor Declan," said Mrs. Ramirez. "¿A dónde vas esta tarde?"

Of all the hall monitors he could have run into, why did it have to be Mrs. Ramirez, he wondered. Like always, she spoke to him in Spanish as if he were still in her class. He barely made it out of Spanish with a C-, and had not spoken a word of the language since the end of sophomore year.

Nervously he stumbled out the words, "Buenas tardes, Señora Ramirez."

For a moment Mrs. Ramirez waited for an answer to her question. When she realized none was coming she repeated, "¿A dónde vas esta tarde?"

Drew had been in a lot of tough situations with adults this year. He questioned the athletic director about who the new indoor coach was. He battled with Mrs. Drain on more than one occasion. The Deuce had cornered him and peppered him with questions. He expertly dissembled to Mr. Peterson about the barrel. Each time he was able to talk his way out of the situation. A fine sheen of nervous sweat appeared on Drew's face. There was no way he was going to get out of this while speaking Spanish.

First he had to figure out the question. *Where are you going this afternoon?*

"Estoy en una excursion a la sala de equipos," he stammered. *I am on an excursion to the equipment room.* "Para cumplir con el gran hombre de equipo." *To meet the big man of equipment.*

Mrs. Ramirez raised an eyebrow. "¿Dónde está tu pase?" she demanded. *Where is your pass?*

"Mi pase es con el hombre del equipo grande," he said weakly. *My pass is with the man of large equipment.*

"If you don't have a pass Drew," said Mrs. Ramirez, switching to English, "You are going to have to go to the main office."

He was running out of options. He had to find that bat or The Deuce would bounce him off the team. There had to be a way to let Mrs. Ramirez let him go.

Drew was a runner at heart, and every runner knows that when the race is its hardest, when it's most painful, that was the time to turn it up and run even harder.

"Tengo una historia," he began tentatively. *I have a story.*

"Es una historia sobre correr, ganar, y Español," he said. *It is a story about running, and winning, and Spanish.*

Mrs. Ramirez was intrigued. She folded her arms across her chest and waited for the story to continue. She was listening.

The Spanish words came to Drew as he started his story. "Este otoño, en el campeonato, estaba cerca de la meta." *This fall, at the championship, I was near the finish.*

"Estaba corriendo tan duro y fue doloroso. Quería rendirme." *I was running so hard and it was painful. I wanted to give up.*

"Entonces oí a un hombre contando. En Español." *Then I heard a man counting. In Spanish.*

"... ocho... nueve... diez." *eight... nine... ten...*

"¡Estaba en décimo lugar!" *I was in tenth place!*

"Seguí adelante con gran aprensión." I went forward with great apprehension.

Mrs. Ramirez tilted her head sideways and frowned. Drew realized his mistake.

"¡No! Con la fortaleza. ¡Corrí con gran fortaleza!" *No! With fortitude. I ran with great fortitude!*

"Corrí duro y terminé décimo." I ran hard and finished tenth.

A slight smile crept to Mrs. Ramirez's face.

To leave no doubt where he was really heading with this story he added, "Fue todo a tu hermosa enseñanza de un robusto español." *It was all to your beautiful teaching of a robust Spanish.*

"Ok, ok, Drew, that's enough," said Mrs. Ramirez. He didn't deserve a better grade than the C- she had given him, but the little Spanish he had retained might help him if he ever needed it. "Next time," she said, opening the door to the back stairwell, "make sure you have a hall pass."

Not wanting to give Mrs. Ramirez a moment to reconsider, Drew clambered down the steps. "Muchas gracias," he called over his shoulder.

Jogging through the tunnel he quickly made it to the main locker room. His plan was to get into the track team locker room and search behind the last row of lockers. Maybe Gil, Casey and Tooch had left the last bat there. That was about where Loganikos was when he destroyed the barrel.

Just as he stepped into the track locker room, Drew heard the voices of two gym teachers walking nearby. Students were not allowed in the team locker rooms during the normal school day. Quickly he snapped the light switch off, throwing the room into darkness, then jumped out of view of the doorway and up onto a bench.

He froze, holding still as he listened to the teachers safely pass by the open door. After a moment he let out a breath of relief, and jumped down off the bench.

A splitting, shearing pain shot up his left ankle. The sound of aluminum grinding on concrete mixed with the primal scream coming from Drew's mouth. He could feel his ankle bone making contact with the floor. The excruciating pain radiated flames of agony around his ankle. Crashing to the floor in a heap, his eyes shut tight, he let out another scream.

His entire conscious mind was focused on the pain, and for two whole seconds not another thought could break through. Pain. Ripping, scorching pain. Then, a small part of his mind was released and tried to figure out what had just happened. He was in the track locker room. It was dark. He jumped off the bench. The sound of aluminum. An aluminum bat rolling on the floor.

Each realization led to another. His left foot had landed on the bat. His ankle had completely rolled over onto the floor. It was severely sprained, maybe even broken. It would take weeks to heal. He had been an athlete for a long time and knew what his body could handle, and what was impossible.

In barely a split second his next thought came through to him clear, certain, and devastating. He could not run in the state meet tomorrow night.

It was over. His senior season was over. The drive for the championship was finished. The team that he put so much heart, soul, and love into was done. His season long—years long—dream would never happen.

Writhing in the darkness on the locker room floor, he let out one more anguished scream.

| 23 |

Bad news travels fast, and by the end of the school day the rest of the guys had heard about Drew's ankle. Some had even seen the ambulance that carted Drew off to the hospital.

At the beginning of practice, the A Set stood in a semicircle around Coach Pilette in a silent stupor. They were only half listening as Coach Pilette rattled off the expected clichés: "It's sad, but expected that injuries happen"; "One runner doesn't make a team"; "Keep focus on your individual race."

Certainly they felt sympathy for Drew. They could imagine themselves in his situation, robbed of a chance to run in the biggest meet of his life. Drew's unrelenting talk about winning a championship, at times annoying, showed how much it meant to him. Now he was going to miss something so important to him. It felt as bad, Casey tried to joke, as having the family dog die.

They were also sorry for themselves. Throughout the season their self confidence had grown with each fast race or long throw. Drew's hype of a championship, laughably outlandish at the beginning of the season, had worked its way into their minds and had become a firm belief. They saw themselves as winners—

as champions. Now that was all in doubt. The odds of winning it all were lower without Drew in the mile and relay.

"How much of a chance do we have without his points?" Gil asked Stats.

Stats shrugged. It was more fun to run the calculations with Drew. "Don't know," he mumbled.

"But there is a chance, right?" insisted Gil.

Anything is possible, thought Stats. "I suppose so," he said unconvincingly.

Workouts the day before a big meet were designed to be very light and effortless. Coach wanted to keep everyone's legs feeling fresh for the following day. But even this reduced workload was too much for the team. The runners were not hitting their times for the intervals, and taking too long on the rests. It was obvious they didn't have the mental energy to focus on running. In what may have been his most decisive moment of the season, Coach Pilette called off the rest of practice and sent the team to the showers early.

Lazer spun around in a few circles before lying down next to Drew's bed. He drew in a large breath then exhaled a heavy, mournful sigh. The old dog needed a rest after all the excitement of the evening. He had watched Drew hobble across the kitchen with aluminum crutches, and with the help of his mother, climb one step at a time up to the bedroom. Lazer heard every word Drew's mother said while trying to console her youngest son.

She told him it could have been worse. The x-rays had come back negative. There were no broken bones, just a severe sprain. A broken bone would have meant a longer recovery time and a cast. With a sprain, he would be able to put his weight on the foot in a few days, and fully recover in a month or so. She said he wouldn't have to miss any school.

Drew wouldn't have any of it. He was down and deflated. He didn't respond to his mother, not a single word. His face was flat and emotionless. Words were useless. Any kind of positive spin his mother could come up with was just not true. His indoor season was over. He couldn't run in the state meet. The dream of a championship was dead. He was devastated, and there wasn't a thing in the world that could pull him out of his self imposed misery.

With his mother back downstairs talking on the phone with his dad in New Jersey, Drew was alone for the first time since he screamed out in pain in the locker room. Lying flat on his back in his bed he stared up at the ceiling above.

His bad ankle, in a soft cast and propped up on a pillow, still throbbed in pain. Even though he hadn't done anything but sit in hospital waiting rooms all afternoon, he was exhausted. If it weren't for the pain and the mental anguish, he would probably slip into a deep sleep.

His mind ran through the events that had brought him to the edge of a championship season. The high mileage weeks of the summer and cross country. Recruiting guys for the indoor team. A new coach. All the tough interval workouts. Fighting that jerk Jeremy. All the craziness with Mrs. Drain. And the stupid bats.

Burning anger hit him when he thought of the aluminum bat that rolled his ankle. He balled his fist and slammed it down on the mattress. "Who left the damn bat on the floor of the locker room?" he shouted.

Lazer sprung to his feet at the outburst.

Drew's anger quickly burned away and left him emotionally spent. After holding it together all afternoon nothing could hide what he felt most deeply, raw sadness. Part of him knew that, in the big scheme of life, a teenage boy missing a race was not a big deal. He would recover and life would go on. But this whole thing—the team, the races, the competition, the chance to do something big—it was important to him. Being a runner, and captain of the team, was how he thought of himself. It was who he was. Without all that, he was nothing—just another kid filling up space in the school hallways. Most of all, he absolutely loved running. And when you lose something you love, you lose part of yourself. Burying his eyes in the crook of his elbow, Drew finally broke. Tears streamed down his cheeks as he sobbed. "It's all over," he croaked.

Violating every rule he had learned since he was a puppy, Lazer summoned his youthful strength and agility, and jumped onto Drew's bed. He laid down, rested his head on Drew's chest, and let out another big, heavy sigh.

Across town there was another River Hawk runner having a pensive evening in his bedroom. Casey sat in a chair hunched over his desk, sketching with a pencil. The gooseneck table lamp threw a tight circle of light in an otherwise dark room. Even though he had the door shut tight the sound of his parents' latest argument seeped into the room.

Guilt mixed with sadness in Casey. He was the one who left the last bat in the locker room. It was going to be a prop for one final "Swing for the Fence" joke. He even thought he might bring the bat on the bus. He never thought anyone would be walking around the locker room during the middle of the school day. Certainly not in the dark.

Dropping his pencil on the desk, he reached for an eraser, made a few touch-ups, then continued sketching with a different pencil. He was in deep focus. He had tuned out the sounds of the argument, and was consumed with his own thoughts. In a way, sketching was a bit like running. It gave your body something to do so your mind could focus on the thoughts that really matted.

He shouldn't have left the bat there. Would Drew be mad at him when he found out? Would the rest of the guys be angry? On the other hand, no one is supposed to be in the locker room. And who walks in a locker room in the pitch black?

The sadness for Drew was real. That guy had put his heart and soul into indoor and now he was out of the biggest meet of his life. Casey still had his senior year to go, but Drew was done. All the talk and hope of a championship was probably done too.

Reaching across the table he grabbed a magazine and flipped through the pages. Finding the photograph that he had in mind, he spread the magazine out next to his sketch pad. The picture was of Steve Prefontaine, the brash, almost mythical hero of every high school runner. Casey had sketched this photo so many times that he could nearly do it from memory. Prefontaine, leaning into a turn on the track, wind rippling through his uniform and hair, muscles flexed on the stride. But it was the look on Prefontaine's face that made him a hero. Determination, toughness, and even a bit of anger. No one could beat Pre, Casey felt, because Pre just wouldn't let them.

Casey had done harm to Drew and to the team, and he wanted to make up for it. He couldn't go back in time and remove the bat. He couldn't fix Drew's ankle. He could only move forward, and run the race of his life tomorrow night. The weight of the world was coming down on him, and he was going to use that power to will his body to run the toughest, best race of his life.

A slight smile came to his face as he inspected his sketch. He had gotten it just right. The track, the body form, the flowing uniform, the illusion of speed and power, it was all perfect. Except there was no mustache on Prefontaine, and there were no early 1970s sideburns either. In fact, it wasn't Prefontaine's face at all. It was Casey's face. He had drawn his own face on the body of the best, toughest, most heroic runner in American history.

Casey stood up with his sketch and walked over to the wall. With a tack, he stuck the sketch among the other sketches on the wall. Rod Dixon beating Geoff Smith in the '83 New York City Marathon. Salazar in front of Beardsley in the Duel in the Sun. Eamonn Coghlan on the boards at the Millrose Games. Steve Jones's world record run in Chicago. All perfectly sketched, and all with Casey's face.

Standing back with his arms crossed, he looked at his work. Casey was ready to run.

In the basement playroom of his family's house Theo Marshall just finished taping off a seven foot diameter circle on the floor. He had planned to use a can of spray paint, but his little sister, Laurell, pointed out that their parents would be mad if he ruined the new wall-to-wall carpet. Duct tape would have to do.

Theo wanted to practice his footwork one more time before tomorrow's meet. With his back to the TV, he crouched down with his toe at the edge of the circle. After a moment of quiet concentration he exhaled out a full breath. Then with surprising quickness for a man his size, he spun around twice, harnessing the centrifugal force, and with a deep, primal scream, launched an imaginary shot into the basement ceiling.

"Foot fault!" yelled Laurell from the couch.

"That wasn't a foul," yelled Theo. "That was the winning throw!"

Laurell raised a skeptical eyebrow then turned her attention back to the TV. Theo was distracting her from her Super Mario game.

"I'm going to keep on doing this until I get my footwork perfect," said Theo.

Time and time again, Theo got into the power position, spun, threw, and maintained his balance.

"What are you up to, T?" asked Mr. Marshall, entering the basement and looking at the tape on the rug. Home late from work and still in his suit, he patiently took in the situation.

"Throwing shot," answered Theo without looking up.

"It's a grapefruit," said Laurell. She was right. He was holding a grapefruit in place of a real shot.

Turning to his dad, Theo said, "Just working on my footwork. The state meet is tomorrow night."

"Yeah, I know," said Mr. Marshall with a smile. Theo had been talking about the meet for weeks. "We are all going to go to watch."

"No!" shouted Laurell. She had no interest in track and did not want to go.

"Yes," said Mr. Marshall emphatically.

"You are going to see history being made," said Theo standing up straight. "The River Hawks are going to bring home a championship."

"Well, now..." said Mr. Marshall with a little skepticism. He knew that the team was going to be missing their fastest miler. "We just want you to do your best. That's all."

"I gotta be better than best, Dad," said a confident Theo. Pointing to his bicep he said, "These arms are strong. These legs got power! I have the balance of a catamount." Raising his voice like a preacher in the pulpit he added, "Great things are going to happen tomorrow night, dad!"

Even Laurell was impressed with the forcefulness of Theo's words.

Mr. Marshall could see the determination in his son, and liked it. "You know T," he said. "I wouldn't bet against you."

Gil sat at the kitchen table surrounded by papers. His mom was used to seeing him do his homework here, but there seemed to be more papers than usual. While cleaning up the dishes from dinner she asked in Portuguese, "Em que tipo de lição de casa você está trabalhando agora?"

"It's not homework, Ma," Gil answered in English. "These are the coaches' reports from all the big teams in tomorrow's meet."

The team relied on Stats to calculate team scoring predictions, and that always bugged Gil. He was the smartest guy on the team, he felt, and Drew and the others should be asking him for the answers. He could do projections and calculations just as well as Stats, just not in his head. He had to write it out on paper. First he organized all the competitor's qualifying times, and then step by step, estimated how those times would result in a team's score. In the state meet the first ten finishers in each event would score points for their team, and his notebook quickly filled up the names of runners from across the state. He wasn't as fast as Stats, but his numbers were more accurate.

"O que você vai fazer com tudo isso?" asked his mom.

Without looking up he said, "I'm trying to figure out how many points we can possibly score in the meet. If we can score enough to win without Drew."

He figured Theo, and Stats would score well, but it was hard to estimate what the rest of the guys would do. He wasn't even sure of what time he would run in the two mile. If he was certain of anything it was that there was no way Casey would beat him. The two had run side by side since freshman year, and Gil was determined to break away from his friend and prove that he was the better runner.

There were so many variables to estimate. Would his teammates run a time consistent with their most recent race, or have a breakthrough day and PR? There was always the chance that they could come out flat, and have a poor run. Who would show up for the competition? The Seacoast teams always seemed to have a runner come out of nowhere and score big.

Gil sat back and tried to make sense of all his tabulations. There were only a few teams in the state that had enough depth to put them into contention, but none of them were the over-whelming favorite. One good race from one runner could push his team to the top.

Earlier in the day he asked Stats if it were possible to win without Drew. Now, having really looked at the numbers himself he knew it was still possible. Possible, but the River Hawks would all have to run their best. He would have to run his best.

"It will probably come down to the relay," he said out loud. The 4 x 440 relay was always the final event of the meet and the last chance for a team to score points. Each team would cobble together their best sprinters, distance, and middle distance guys, and see if they could string together a few decent quarter miles.

"Você faz parte da equipe de revezamento?" asked his mother.

"Yeah, I'm on the relay," answered Gil. "Along with Casey, the new kid from the basketball team, and..." He trailed off. Who will fill Drew's spot as the anchor of the relay? Constantine? Little Tooch? Stats wouldn't run more than 200 yards. God forbid, Loganikos, or Theo. Could anyone fill Drew's spot? "I don't think we have a fourth guy."

That didn't seem possible to his mother. "O treinador terá que escolher alguém."

"Yeah, I guess Coach will tell us when we get there," said Gil. Whoever it is, he thought, they better have the run of their life.

Stats and his mother were watching TV in their apartment when the doorbell buzzed. It was unusual to have someone coming around on a weeknight, but not unheard of. "Who's there now, do you think?" asked his mom.

"Don't know," said Stats, getting up and heading into the apartment hallway. Before opening the door, he looked through the peephole, and recognized Keith.

Even though they lived in the same building they had not seen much of each other since Keith quit the team. They left for school at different times, didn't have any of the same classes, and Stats's afternoons were filled up with track practice. On weekends Stats would rather hang out with other friends than get mixed up in whatever Keith had going on.

"Hey," said Stats flatly when he opened the door. There were a few other guys with Keith in the hallway who weren't from around the neighborhood.

"Say, bro," began Keith. "Haven't seen you around much. Where have you been?"

Stats shrugged his shoulders. "Been around, like usual."

One of the other guys whacked Keith on the arm and nodded toward Stats. They had obviously come to get something from Stats.

From the living room Stats's mother called out, "Who's there, Donell?"

"It's Keith. It's all right," he answered.

"Well, have him come on in, then," she said.

Stats ignored his mother. He wasn't letting Keith and these guys into his home. "What do you want?" he asked Keith.

"We're going to go out. Have some fun. Get a little business done, you know," said Keith. "Get your shoes."

Stats wasn't one hundred percent certain what kind of business Keith was talking about, but if it was in the same line of work as Jeremy Lamonda was in, he didn't want any part of it. Being expelled and arrested wasn't part of his life's plan.

Shaking his head he said, "No. I've got something big going on tomorrow. Have to rest to be the best."

Keith scoffed, "What do you have going on that's so big?" He stepped forward right up to the threshold to the door. "Bigger than being with your friends? Don't be a momma's boy."

Stats chuckled. It had nothing to do with his mother. It was about something he wanted to do. To be the best. He had skills other people didn't have and he was going to use them to get ahead. Keith wasn't going to intimidate him. Standing up straight he looked his cousin in the eye and said, "No. I ain't going. I got something big going on tomorrow, you know what I'm saying."

Keith shook his head disgustedly. "It better be important, because we're not going to forget."

The veiled threat just made Stats more confident. Nothing was going to stop him from running great tomorrow night. "Yeah. It's important," he said right before he closed the door.

Sitting in the back room of his parent's restaurant, Tooch and his grandmother were finishing up a late dinner. After school and into the evening Tooch spent hours at Heng Khmer doing his homework and waiting for his parents. His grandmother didn't have much to do with operating the restaurant anymore, but still liked being there surrounded by her family.

"Yiey," Tooch addressed his grandmother, "what was Taa like?" The question was a bit out of the blue since they mostly talked about day-to-day things like school, the restaurant, and his running. Over the years he had heard stories about Taa, his grandfather, and right now he wanted to know more. "You always said that he was brave, and all that. But was he tough?"

It only took his grandmother a moment to get over the surprise of the topic. She didn't often talk about her late husband. "Brave, yes. Tough? I guess you could say that. He did what was best for his family, even in the toughest times," she answered thoughtfully. "Why do you ask?"

"I know all the things he did during the war, and getting us here," he said, summarizing years of displacement, refugee camps, and immigration in a few vague words. "And I was thinking, if he was tough, or brave, then maybe I am too. Maybe I can be like that too."

"Ah," she said. Now she understood what the conversation was about. "Well, that was a different time. Things are much better here," she said. Getting to the point she added, "I think you do have those qualities. You have helped yourself get here too. You've done the schoolwork. You learned the language. No one else did that for you. You did it."

Tooch wasn't convinced yet. "Yeah, but I had to do those things. I'm talking about things I'm not sure I can do," he said. "Like tomorrow. What if I'm weak, and run bad? What if I ruin it for everyone?"

"You put too much pressure on yourself. Maybe you are like Taa," she observed. Her grandson seemed anxious and unsettled, and she tried to put him at ease. "You are so fast. You've run all those miles in training. You will do well."

"I have to run fast," insisted Tooch. "I can't let him. . . everyone down. I have to run my best race, ever."

"Sounds like you are determined," she said. "Strength of the mind is as important as strength of muscles. I think your Taa would like that."

"I am not going to let them down," Tooch repeated emphatically.

Lazer raised an eyebrow but didn't move a muscle when Drew's mom burst into the bedroom. He was still curled up to his master on the bed. Drew had stopped crying a while before, but Lazer felt that he was still needed right there next to his master.

"I've got exciting news," she said in a sing-song voice. She paused, waiting for Drew to ask what the exciting news was, but after several silent moments she continued on her own. "Julia's contractions have started and they are headed to the hospital."

"Oh," said Drew flatly. He was happy for his brother and Julia, and he was even a bit excited to be an uncle, but right now none of those emotions could break through his misery.

"No telling how long it could take," continued his mother. "Could be later tonight. Could be sometime tomorrow. Dad better make it back from New Jersey."

"Yeah," said Drew. He hadn't moved a muscle, still laying on his back looking at the ceiling.

His mother wasn't getting the joyful feedback she was expecting. "Well, I'm sure we will all be making a visit to the hospital tomorrow evening."

This caught Drew's attention. "What? All of us? To the hospital? Tomorrow?" he repeated back. "No, I can't go tomorrow. I still have the track meet," he said.

She raised her eyebrows in doubt and nodded toward his soft cast. "You obviously can't run," she said. In an exasperated voice she added, "You know, you are going to be an uncle a lot longer than you'll be on this team."

Drew sat up and swung his feet to the floor. Lazer jumped down to get out of the way. "Yeah," he agreed testily. The admonishment from his mom; that what his older brother was doing was more important than what Drew was doing, brought out his competitiveness. "That's right. I've got one more day. I'm still the captain, and I'm still part of the team, you know."

Gone was the sadness and self pity. His drive for a championship wasn't about him anymore. Sure, he had recruited, encouraged, and managed these guys all season to help him win a championship, but they deserved it more than him. The guys had all bought into the dream. They had done the training, believed in themselves, and placed themselves on the threshold of a championship. It was about them now. Stats, Tooch, Gil, Casey and the others weren't just points on his tally sheet, they were his friends. His River Hawk brothers. Even on one leg he had to help them win.

"I'm not going to the hospital tomorrow," he said. His injured ankle was just one more obstacle, one more challenge to be overcome. He stood on his good foot and looked at his mother. "I'm going to the state meet tomorrow night with the River Hawks. I can't be a champion this season, but we can."

| 24 |

The Gut Run Drew survived his freshman year taught him how to hold the pace and keep going when the body was begging for rest. All the long, hard runs and training he had run since made him a faster and stronger athlete, and he prided himself on his endurance. So it was humbling to find that hobbling along with his crutches for the shortest walk in the school hallways was so exhausting.

"I don't think you can even make it up the stairs of the bus tonight with those things," teased Monique. Like a true friend she volunteered to carry Drew's books from class to class.

"I'm glad you have such confidence in me," Drew replied dryly. His face had a light shine of perspiration from the effort.

The crutches' aluminum tubes made a "thwack" sound every time he planted them for his next swing. Students stopped what they were doing to watch as he swung down the hall. Kids had been offering condolences to him all morning, and by the second period he had grown tired of retelling the story of his injury. It was nice to have Monique with him because her presence kept them from asking the same questions.

"Why are you even going?" she asked. It seemed like the smart thing to do with a badly sprained ankle was rest, not hop around The Oaks. "You can't do anything at the meet," she said emphasizing the word "do." He obviously couldn't run, so why go?

"What do you want me to do," he said continuing with the sarcasm, "sit at home and watch Chariots of Fire again?"

"What's that? Some kind of gladiator movie?" she asked without a hint of recognition.

"Never mind." It would take too long to explain what he liked about the decade old running movie. "I'm still on the team, and I have to be there. There's still a chance we could win, and if we do I want to be part of it." After the talk with his mom and a night's sleep, Drew had returned to his more positive, confident manner. He couldn't run, but he was sure that somehow he could still help his team.

"Yeah, well, you'll have to get yourself on that bus 'cause I'll be on the girls' bus. We got the whole big bus to ourselves, and we're leaving early," said Monique.

Drew swung to a stop in front of his last class of the day, and took his notebook from Monique. "See you at The Oaks," he said.

There was little talk in the locker room that afternoon. The guys were quietly changing from their street clothes into their uniforms. The long walk through the tunnel to the track locker room had been exhausting so Drew just sat in front of his locker wearing his River Hawks jacket. He couldn't quite gauge the mood of the room. Were they melancholy at the loss of a chance to win the meet? Or maybe they were all over that and were just focusing on their own performances. Either way, the mood was certainly unsettled.

If Coach Pilette were here he might try to give a speech that would get the team motivated, he thought. Then he chuckled to himself. Any speech from Coach would probably have the opposite effect. Maybe it was up to him to say something that would get the guys pumped up, but frankly he didn't know what to say.

In the midst of the quiet, JB entered the locker room talking a mile a minute.

"You know what you guys need?" he asked the room. It wasn't a real question. He wasn't expecting a response from anyone. He answered his own question. "You need a trainer. One with experience. River Hawk experience. No team has ever won a championship without a trainer. That's what my dad says, "All good teams need a good trainer," he said. That's why I'm a trainer. 'Cause teams need trainers. Good ones. Especially River Hawks. That's what you need. A trainer."

Tension in the room evaporated, and there were smiles on the guys faces. It was probably the first time in history that someone tried to talk their way *onto* the indoor track team.

"You're right, JB," said Drew. "We need a guy like you to help us tonight." How could anyone resist the childlike enthusiasm of the River Hawks biggest fan. "Will you be our trainer?"

"What? Me?" asked JB. "Ok, I can do that. I can be the trainer. You guys really need me, 'cause you need all the help you can get," he added bluntly.

"Hold on," said Stats. Walking up to JB he said, "Can't have a trainer wearing a basketball jacket. This here is a track team, you know what I'm saying?"

JB's face fell. It looked like he was about to burst into tears. Drew was stunned. What kind of jerk could say no to JB?

Theo couldn't believe what he was hearing. The feud between the two football players had been simmering under the surface all season, and Theo was about to rip it wide open. Muscles clenched, he stood up and started for Sats.

In the same instant Stats unzipped his own jacket. With a big smile he said, "You'll have to wear my jacket." He draped his River Hawks running jacket over JB's shoulders. "Now, what we have here," he announced to the team, "is a real-life track team trainer."

And just like that the good mood returned to the locker room. Theo relaxed. He never expected Stats to be so kind-hearted. The guys stood around JB and gave high fives to their new teammate.

"So, what exactly does a track team trainer do?" asked Casey lightheartedly. "I mean, do you have specific responsibilities?"

"I tell the team when the bus is here," said JB. "I make sure everyone knows, so they can get on the bus. I let the guys know."

"Ok," said Drew. "So, you will let us know when the bus gets here."

"Yeah." said JB. He paused for a moment, then announced, "The bus is here."

"Our bus?"

"Yeah. It's been here for twenty minutes," said JB. "That's why you guys needed a trainer, 'cause you didn't know that your bus was here."

At the same time Theo and Stats yelled, "Let's go!"

Rather than spreading out among the empty rows of seats, the guys packed together near the front of the short bus, and despite the fewer rows it still felt empty. Had the girl's team been there it would have been a tight fit. Drew made it up the stairs without a problem but was still glad to plop down in the first row.

"We have a problem. We have a big problem," said JB. He had quickly switched pronouns to include himself on the team. "We don't have a coach."

Where was Coach Pilette? No one had given him a thought. He had never entered the locker room the whole season, so no one missed him there. He was normally the first one on the bus talking with the driver.

"Where is he?" asked Gil. "We have to go soon."

"What is he—just running late?" wondered Casey.

"He's not coming," said JB. "His pager went off and he left. He called from the hospital. I was in the office when he called."

Drew was incredulous. "What do you mean he's not coming?"

"From the hospital?" asked Gil.

"From the hospital," answered JB. "He called from the hos-pital. He's having a baby. Today's the day for his baby, and he's at the hospital, and he's not coming."

"Can't he do that some other day?" asked Tooch.

Drew's brother and sister-in-law were also at the hospital having a baby. They had been in the same birthing class as

Coach Pilette and his wife. What were the odds that they would have a baby on the same day? And why did it have to happen on the day of the state championship?

Having a baby and starting a family was probably the biggest, most important part of life, Drew had to admit. He knew how much it meant to Greg and Julia, and he bet Coach Pilette and his wife were no different. There was no way Coach would miss the birth of his first child, he thought. It was definitely more important than coaching a bunch of kids at a high school track meet.

"It's getting late," said Gil. "We have to leave soon."

"No coach, no go. This bus isn't going to move without a coach," said Stats.

"How are we going to find another coach?" asked Tooch. "And find him now?"

The guys all looked at Drew. Time and time again this season Drew had come up with a plan, or a solution, or just some way to get the team ready. He had been able to clear a path through all the craziness and chaos that the team had run into this season. Now they expected him to come through again.

A wave of doubt washed over him. This may be the thing that finally stopped them. A roadblock with no way around. Kids don't normally find replacement coaches for their own teams.

"What are you all looking at me for?" he yelled. He could never have anticipated the coach not showing up. "Why don't you guys think of something?"

Silence filled the bus as the guys looked at each other cluelessly. Everything had always been taken care of for them by adults, and they weren't used to acting on their own.

After a few moments Tooch offered, "What about Coach DeLuca?"

"The girls' bus already left," said Gil, shooting down the idea.

Shrugging his shoulders Casey weakly added, "We don't have an assistant coach." The spring outdoor track team often had an assistant coach to help with the field events, but not indoor.

The few ideas they had were quickly exhausted. With the team at a loss of what to do, it grew agonizingly quiet on the bus.

Being a runner, especially a distance runner, Drew was used to pushing his body past what he thought was possible. In a race, facing pain and exhaustion, he could still find another gear and run on. When the pain was at its worst, his mind would focus on the things that mattered: don't stop; keep on running; never give up.

He couldn't run tonight, but he was still the captain. It was still his team. He still had to lead them. This was the most important thing in the world to him, and he had to find a solution.

"You know," he started. "There's probably only one person who wants Aiken High to win a championship more than I do."

"At track?" Casey asked skeptically.

"No. At anything," said Drew. "Anything River Hawk. And he's been waiting for thirty years to get another chance at a state championship." Standing up and grabbing his crutches, he said, "Let's go see The Deuce."

The weeks between the winter and spring sports seasons were usually a slow, and, frankly, boring time of the year for The Deuce. Having already collected the gear from the hockey and basketball teams, there wasn't much to do until he started handing out the bats and balls for baseball. While there was probably some paperwork he should be working on, he used the quiet time in his office to reread a paperback copy of *The Godfather*.

When he heard a commotion outside the equipment room he assumed it was another fist fight, but that didn't quite make sense. There were so few students in the school at this time of day, and the only two teams still competing, the two track teams, had already left on their buses. He didn't know whether to be relieved or annoyed when Drew Declan and the rest of the team poured into his office.

"Hey, Mr. Martin. We need your help," said Drew as the team crowded around him in the doorway.

"My help?" asked The Deuce. Crossing his arms and leaning back in his chair he asked, "What? Did one of you get a stain on your nice, new tracksuits?"

Ignoring the dig, Drew went on to explain. "Coach Pilette is at the hospital having a baby. The girls' bus already left. We need a coach to take us to the state meet. So..." he paused looking at his teammates, "we're asking if you can be our coach tonight."

"Ha, well..." The Deuce was caught off guard. He had seen kids ask for some crazy things over the years but this Declan kid was something else. "Kids—no..." said The Deuce, shaking his head. His first thought went to the administrative and legal red tape one normally has to go through to be named a head coach. "It doesn't really work that way. I wouldn't be..." Then reconsidering, he figured since he was technically part of the athletic department, would it really be so wrong if he helped out a team when they needed it? And since when did he care about the administration's red tape? For years he had been trying to work his way back onto the football coaching staff without any luck. Coaching track had never crossed his mind, until now.

"No. I don't know anything about. . .," he stammered. He had never organized a track workout in his life. He wouldn't even know what to do with himself at a state track meet. "I mean, who's even in the starting line up?"

"The roster has already been submitted," Gil assured him. "We know what we're running."

"This was Coach Pilette's first year," reminded Casey. "None of the officials know what he looks like. You'll fit right in."

"This is crazy. I can't see how..." The Deuce started to demure.

"We need a coach to lead the way," interrupted Drew. "We need you."

The Deuce didn't reply right away. The possibilities whirled around his mind.

"This is our best chance, our last chance to be champions," said Drew. The Deuce needed convincing and Drew was going to play to his soft spot. "Some of us may never run for the River Hawks again. We don't want to go the rest of our lives knowing we were just a yard short of a championship."

The Deuce was listening now. He had been one yard short of a championship when he was in high school, and not a season had gone by without him thinking about it.

"This team will be champions tonight," continued Drew. "We've got guys with speed. Guys with endurance. Guys who can throw. Heck, we even have a guy who can jump 6'8" if he wants to. We have the depth to score enough points and win." He stretched out his crutches and swung a step closer to The Deuce.

"The guys on this team come from all over Aiken. Some of us live in the development, some of us live in the Beech Hill Estates. We got guys who are still learning English, and guys whose families have been here for two hundred years." Drew took in a breath, getting ready to deliver his finish. "But tonight none of that makes a difference. Tonight we are a team, united with one purpose. To win a championship for the River Hawks."

"This is important to all of us, and when something is important it is ok to put all your effort, all your passion, and all your hopes into it. Right now we need a leader who has been there, who knows how much effort you have to give, how you would do anything to help your teammates win, and how these moments in life matter. Someone who knows what it really means to be a River Hawk."

The Deuce blinked. Drew's words were awakening a passion that had been dormant in his heart for over fifteen years.

"We are the River Hawks," continued Drew, "the fastest, toughest, strongest team in the state. We have one goal. Tonight we are going to show everyone what we know to be true: River Hawks run!"

Fifteen years of pent up frustration poured out of The Deuce. The love he had for the games, the kids and for the thrill of winning burst forth. The Deuce jumped up, knocking the novel to the floor. With his eyes wide open he raised one fist in the air and shouted, "Let's run, River Hawks!"

The parking lot at The Oaks Burgett Track and Community Center was just about full when the River Hawks' bus rolled in, and they had to park on the far side of the lot. Since the two mile was the first event of the meet, Casey and Gil bolted off the bus the minute the door opened for their warmup run in the neighborhood. The rest of the team gathered up their bags and started the long walk toward the giant bronze statue of Oaks swinging his baseball bat.

Walking across the lot Theo caught up with Stats. "Hey, that was cool what you did back there," he said.

"What was cool?" asked Stats.

"Giving your jacket to JB," said Theo. "At first, I was going to rip your head off, but then I was like, 'Hey, that's real cool.'"

"Rip my head off?" asked Stats playfully. "You'll never be fast enough to catch me, you know what I'm saying."

They both laughed. Then Stats added, "But you're going to lose your jacket too."

"What? No one's taking my River Hawk colors," said Theo, balling a fist.

"Yo, you'll be giving it away," answered Stats. "Our new coach needs a jacket." The Deuce needed a track jacket to fit in with the team.

"Why me?" asked Theo.

"You the only one big enough," said Stats. "The Deuce is all big and frumpy. The man needs a big jacket."

"Damn," agreed Theo.

The team found an empty spot high in the crowded stands to stow their gear. Drew slowly made his way up the stairs with his crutches, followed by The Deuce who was covered with a thick layer of perspiration from the effort. The first-time coach was taking his role seriously and started barking out orders. "Listen up, guys. This is our headquarters. Substitutes will sit here on the bench and check in when called." Looking at a roster on a clipboard he announced, "Jason and Gilberto are up first. Get ready."

The names were unfamiliar to most of the guys. "Who's that?" asked Stats.

"Casey and Gil," answered Drew matter of factly.

Theo couldn't believe it. "Jason?" he asked. "I always thought Casey was his first name."

Drew redirected the conversation back to The Deuce. "Coach, they are already warming up for their race. We actually like to move around The Oaks a lot because the events start at different spots all around the track," he said. Thinking that he needed to stay close to The Deuce to make sure the novice didn't say the wrong thing to an official and blow their cover, he added, "But you should stay up here in the stands." Soon the guys started to split up as they got ready for their events.

Through the first twelve laps of the two mile, Gil and Casey ran comfortably with the lead pack. When the top runners made a push, Gil tried to match the move and open a gap on Casey. With three laps to go both runners had fallen further back in the field, and were struggling to maintain the pace. Finishing side by side once again, they had run well but disappointingly, placed outside the top ten, and scored no points. Normally running a PR in a state meet would make them happy, but with no points to show for their effort they were crestfallen. To make matters worse, Runner Ten from Seacoast had the race of his life and finished first, scoring ten points.

They wore blank stares of disappointment when they made it back to headquarters. The Deuce wrapped his arms around their shoulders and tried to console them. "Hell of a race, boys. You left it all out there." They didn't acknowledge the remark, so he added, "You had a great season, and you'll be back stronger next year."

"Oh, we're not done," said Casey, snapping out of his funk.

"Yeah," agreed Gil. "We're still running the relay, and we'll be ready."

JB came up the stands to report on the field events. "Captain Marshall is in third," he said. "Third place so far. His first two throws put him in the top three. One more. He has one more chance to throw." Switching gears he reported on the 50. "Captain Stats is in the final. The final heat. We have to watch him."

Stats's time in the preliminary heats was the fastest of all sprinters, and that placed him in the middle lane for the final. Far on the outside lane was his most important competition, a runner from the Seacoast Wave. The runners in the closer lanes had run better times and were more likely to contend for the win, but the real battle was to score more points than the Wave.

The crowd of spectators and athletes turned their attention to the infield lanes where the sprinters lined up in their lanes. Conversations stopped and the gymnasium became still. At the starter's command the racers bent down and settled into their blocks. Anticipation for the fastest and most explosive race of the day hung in the air. Except for the hum of the lights The

Oaks was dead silent. On the "set" command the sprinters raised up in their blocks, focused on reacting to the starter's gun.

Cutting through the tension, from the top of the stands, a man screamed, "Let's run River Hawks!" The starter called for the runners to stand up. The entire crowd turned and looked at The Deuce. Drew covered his own face with his hands.

From the set command to the finish it takes about six seconds for the 50 to be run, and each second is its own story. On the gun, Stats shot out of the blocks and accelerated up to full speed. At fifteen yards he had a half stride lead on the field. For the next ten yards the sprinters ran in unison, maintaining their formation, speed and place. Starting at thirty yards a taller runner in the third lane used his long strides to steadily move up and pass Stats for the lead. Down the final ten yards Stats, still holding onto second place, gave one more burst of speed, and leaned into the finish line.

"Oh, no," The Deuce said crestfallen. "He lost."

"He didn't lose," corrected Drew. "He came in second, and scored eight points. And..." he paused to make his point, "Seacoast finished out of the scoring. So we're back in it."

The Deuce's outburst at the start of the 50 yard final had attracted attention. A coach from another team wandered up the stands to give Drew his condolences for not being able to run. Thin, lean, and wearing his team's running jacket, the gray-haired coach still looked like he could jump on the track and run a few laps with his team. He had been coaching high school track long enough to know many of the top runners and almost all of the other coaches. "Don't worry Drew," said the coach. "You will have a great outdoor season." Turning to The

Deuce with bewilderment in his voice he asked, "You must be Coach Pilette?"

Without a moment's pause The Deuce answered, "Yup. Coach Pilette. Nice to meet ya."

Unconvinced, the coach continued his line of questioning, "The same Ethan Pilette who won the '91 Ivy League 5,000?"

The Deuce straightened back his shoulders, sucked in his gut as much as he could and emphatically answered, "Yes. Yes I am." He ended the conversation by walking past the coach and yelling out a command, "Round up the team and get a point tally. We got a meet to win, here."

Through the first three hurdles of the 55 yard hurdles final Constantine was running the race of his life. He had the perfect three-step cadence between hurdles that Coach Pilette had preached all season. His newfound fluidity, along with his natural speed, put Constantine—Constantine!—in the lead by a half a stride.

"Who is this guy?" shouted Drew. It was like another runner snuck into Constantine's body. That their teammate was stepping up to the challenge and looking like he was going to score a lot of points was a shock. Drew was stunned that it was Constantine the goofball, of all people, who was making up the slack caused by his injury. It would be humiliating for Drew if Constantine could claim to be the better athlete.

Inexplicably, between the third and fourth hurdles Constantine switched back to four steps, and led with his non-dominant leg. The change ruined his rhythm and slightly threw him off stride. Trying to maintain his balance, panic filled Constantine and he stuttered-stepped five steps between four and five. The rest of the field, still smooth in their technique, gained ground on him at the last hurdle. It was Constantine's trailing foot that hit the fifth hurdle, not hard enough to knock it over, but with just enough impact to twist his upper body on the landing. At a slower speed he may have been able to recover his balance, and maintain his momentum. But Constantine had been bold, and ran his race with as much speed as he could muster. All of his energy and strength had been spent. Over the last seven steps to the finish line, and possibly scoring points for his team, he wobbled, awkwardly throwing his arms out to maintain his balance. With a final lunge, Constantine landed face down on the rubberized floor just past the finish line. The possibility of victory, so plausible a mere second earlier, has been replaced with the shocking reality of failure. He finished out of the scoring. It was one brief moment in a lifetime, but one Constantine would regretfully look back on for the rest of his life.

Traitor ran unexpectedly well in the 600, finishing seventh. The points he scored didn't make up for Constantine's collapse, but it helped the River Hawks stay close to Seacoast. Glad that the team got some needed points, Drew was still irked that a non-runner like Traitor could do so well. With so little track training, Traitor walked on mid-season and still beat just about everyone in the state. There were so many talented athletes out there wasting their time in other sports, Drew thought. If they only focused on track, his River Hawks would be a powerhouse.

It was Tooch's inexperience running in a crowded field that ruined his race. On the first lap he went out with the pack and found himself in lane one, boxed in. With no room to maneuver and run his normal pace, Tooch was trapped in the thicket of slower runners through the sixth lap. Desperate to get to an outside lane, he slowed his pace and swung around the runners in lane two. With a lap and a half to go he finally broke free and got up to full speed. By then he was too far behind the leaders to have any impact on the race, and even with a strong kick, he finished far behind and, more frustratingly, out of the scoring.

Up in the stands the River Hawks regrouped to figure out their scoring situation. "Well, you guys put up a good fight, and you should be proud of yourselves," said The Deuce while shuffling through a bunch of race results on his clipboard. "There's no shame in doing your best."

The guys looked confused. "Coach, the meet's not over," said Gil.

"Look son," said The Deuce. "I know you all did your best, but Seacoast has a lead, and without Drew's points in the mile..." He trailed off, implying that the team didn't have any runners left that could score.

"Numbers are numbers." said Stats shaking his head. "Even if T wins the shot, we're still behind Seacoast."

"No. That's not true," said Gil quietly. "I've been keeping track of the points too, and I think there is still a chance."

Pissed off that someone would dare challenge his math skills, Stats stood up to face Gil. "Where are you getting off with that! You can't do two plus two!"

"Math is math," said Gil standing up and holding up his own clipboard.

Drew put his crutch in-between the two. "Hey! Will you guys back off." Then turning to Gil he asked, "What do you got?"

"They didn't score any points in the mile since they had their best runner in the two," said Gil. "If Theo wins the shot, that puts us within two points."

"But we're still down by two," said Stats. That was the same number he came up with in his head.

Drew was catching on to Gil's line of thinking. "It's not about how many points we've scored so far," he said. "It's about how many we can score from here on."

The Deuce waved his clipboard in the air. "Hello! All of our runners are done," he said with heavy sarcasm.

"So we just have to beat them in the relay," answered Drew. The relay is always the last event of a track meet.

"Relay?" asked Stats. "We've never run a fast time in the relay. And Drew ain't running."

"We'll just have to put together a better team," said Drew. Seeing Stats's skepticism he added, "That's what River Hawks do."

"But first," broke in Casey. "Theo has to win. Let's go tell him."

The guys started to shuffle down the grandstands when Stats spoke up. "No. Hold up," he said. "I'll tell him. Y'all stay up here." Then to lighten the mood a bit he turned to Gil and joked, "You just keep your pencils sharp."

Stats found Theo in the shot put holding area and laid out the math. Theo had to win to put the River Hawks relay team within striking distance. Theo's stone-face expression didn't change, but Stats could tell that the big man was feeling the pressure.

"Hey. Who's going to beat you? No one," Stats said encouragingly. "You're the champion. You're the biggest, strongest mother in this whole building. In this whole state! You're gonna throw that thing straight out the window and smack Oaks Burgett upside the head. You know what I'm saying."

"Yeah," answered Theo. "I know what you are saying." With his confidence building he added, "I am going to get in the ring, and utterly crush it."

Maybe it was the talk he had with Stats. Maybe it was the extra footwork practice he had done the night before. Maybe it was his own pride, his own desire to be the best, to be a champion. Most likely it was all of these things. Theo Marshall stepped into the shot ring, crouched into his starting position, and let out a deep breath. For a moment he was motionless, focusing his attention on harnessing all of his strength. In a burst of energy, Theo spun across the ring and reached the power position. With a deep, powerful scream, he launched an absolute rocket. The flight path of the shot arced high over the floor in a perfect parabola. Watching from the sideline other throwers yelled out in shock and surprise, as if they were witnessing the end of gravity. With a heavy thud the shot landed far beyond any of the other scuff marks on the floor. Theo Marshall left no doubt who was champion.

Back in the stands, The Deuce called the team in for another meeting. "We are right where we have to be," he started. "We're in contention. We are in striking position!" The Deuce was in his element—leading a team in the final moments of a close game. "Now, we don't have to win the whole relay. We just have to stay in front of Seacoast." Then he repeated himself to make sure the simple fact got through: "Stay in front of Seacoast."

"Hey coach," broke in Gil. "Who's on the relay?"

"Yeah," concurred Casey, "With Constantine bashed up from the hurdles, and Drew's ankle, who's going to run?"

The Deuce's face fell. He had no idea who was going to run. He didn't know half of the guys on the team. "Ah, well," he stammered. "In the long tradition of the River Hawks," he paused, trying to think of an answer. "The team captain always decides." As the whole team, once again turned to Drew, The Deuce held out his clipboard and said, "Captain, what's your lineup?"

This time Drew was not caught by surprise. He had been thinking of the perfect relay team all day, and didn't hesitate to give out the assignments.

"We have to get out fast to match up with their best sprinter," he began. Turning to his co-captain he said, "Stats, you are going to take the first leg."

"What? No!" shouted Stats. "A quarter mile? No. I run a 50 yard race. In football, I never run longer than 100 yards. Two hundred yards in a workout is, like, long distance for me. A quarter mile? No."

"This isn't football," countered Drew. "It's track, and we need runners. Fast guys like you."

Stats shook his head as if he was trying to make up his mind.

With a firm and commanding voice The Deuce wished he had, Drew continued, "You are going to run the first leg. You are going to go out with the leaders, and you are going to hang on for as long as you can."

Stats let out a groan. He took a deep breath as he accepted the challenge. "Who do I hand off to?" he asked.

Drew spun and pointed at Gil. "Gil," he said. "You're going to get the baton ahead of Seacoast. All you have to do is run your race and stay ahead of them."

"Hey, during your exchange," said Casey to the first two runners, "You won't have time to argue over point totals."

"Casey," said Drew sharply. He wasn't in the mood to joke around and wanted the team to be focused. "You have to run a great race. You have to open the gap on Seacoast as much as you can."

"Ok," said Casey seriously. "Who do I hand off to?"

The logical answer would have been Traitor. He had good middle distance speed, and had just come off an impressive 600 yard run. The kid was a good athlete, and could probably run well. But Drew didn't want just any athlete anchoring the relay. He wanted a real runner. Someone who understood how to push himself to the limit when he was the most tired. Someone who felt the weight of his whole team on his shoulders. He wanted an anchor who understood that this was not just another play in a game. It was the most important run of their lives. A run for a championship.

"Tooch," said Drew. "You're our anchor."

Tooch was shocked. His eyes went wide as the implication of the task sank in.

The other guys were also surprised. Traitor was visibly disappointed. For a moment it looked like The Deuce was going to intercede and put Traitor back on the relay, but before he could say anything Stats stepped forward.

"Give it here, Anchorman," said Stats, reaching a hand out to Tooch. "You going to bring us home the final 440." The two teammates clasped hands. With Stats's approval, the lineup for the relay was settled. The Deuce wasn't going to overrule two team captains. Traitor turned and walked away as the rest of the guys crowded around the four relay runners.

"All hands in, yo!" yelled Stats. Everyone reached a hand in and put it on one another's. "Nice and loud," commanded Stats. "What do River Hawks do?"

"River Hawks run!" they shouted.

There were ten teams in the 4x440 relay and by looking at the season long results the Boston Engineering Academy Blazers were the heavy favorite. They had two guys who could run a sub :50 440 and two other strong runners. But they didn't matter because the Blazers weren't close in the team scoring. What mattered was the third seed team, the Seacoast Wave, in lane two, and the fifth seed team, the Aiken River Hawks in lane three.

While Gil and Stats continued to argue about the exact point totals of the two teams, and how many points were still up for grabs, both agreed that the relay would put either team over the top.

Word had gotten around The Oaks about the team showdown in the relay. The River Hawks girls' team lined up along the far straightaway. A crowd of spectators collected near the finish line ready to watch the confusion of the transition zone, and hopefully see a close race.

Drew wanted his four runners to practice a few handoffs, but each guy was so focused on their upcoming run that he couldn't get them to do it. Stats made his way to the starting line holding the baton like he held the football last fall.

The starter called set, then fired the gun. Stats and two others shot out to the lead before they hit the back straightaway. The Deuce was jumping up and down and yelling as Stats ran by the far turn. Through the first 220 Stats looked strong, holding on to the third spot, well ahead of the Seacoast runner in seventh. But as he predicted, heading into the final 100 of his leg, Stats started to tighten up. His head tilted back, his shoulders were tense, and his stride shortened. Two runners moved past him on the final turn. Heading into his final straightaway he recovered some and muscled it out, holding off any other runners.

Gil grabbed the baton two places ahead of Seacoast. The Seacoast runner sprinted out of the transition zone and caught up to Gil at the top of the first back stretch. Gil didn't panic. He was an experienced racer and knew he was on the right pace. Coming through the first 220 Seacoast stayed even with Gil and into the turn they were stride for stride. Gil's strength started to pay off and he pulled forward along the back stretch. The Seacoast runner had gone out too fast in trying to catch up to Gil, had used up all of his strength, and was fading. Gil looked like he could run a few more laps at this pace.

The gym was electric with excitement. Since no one was allowed in the middle of the track while the field events were going on, the two teams lined the edge of the track screaming and cheering for their teams. Other runners, normally indifferent to a race they were not part of, gathered around to spectate an exciting finish.

Gil was moving so well it took Casey by surprise. As his teammate approached the transition zone, Casey accelerated into his pace, and then turned to reach back for the baton. Gil, still running fast, had closed the gap between the two and held the baton out forward. When Casey's arm swung back for the handoff his elbow hit the top of the baton, knocking it from Gil's hand down to the track.

The Deuce shrieked. Drew put his head in his hands. Stats threw his head back.

Casey came to a complete stop, bent down and grabbed the baton. Three teams passed him before he started running again. By the time he got up to speed he was a good five yards behind Seacoast.

On the sidelines the team was dejected. A five yard gap over a 440-yard race would be tough to overcome. Drew had hoped the team would get to the anchor leg with a lead so Tooch could hold on as the Seacoast's best runner tried to catch him, but now none of that looked likely. It was too much to ask Tooch, just a sophomore, to run down and catch Seacoast. The entire season, the whole dream of being champions had been knocked to the floor with the baton. The team stood in silence watching Casey's leg of the race.

Even though he was frustrated and upset, Casey had enough experience to know that he shouldn't sprint after Seacoast to close the gap early. He had just seen the second leg of Seacoast do just that: race out to catch Gil, but fade weakly over the last 100. After getting over the shock of the drop, Casey quickly made a plan: try to maintain the gap - or even close it a bit- then unleash his closing kick and catch Seacoast at the handoff.

The guys watched quietly as Seacoast and Casey went through the 220. Drew thought that if Casey were here on the sidelines watching a similar race he probably would have come up with a joke to break the tension. Drew tried, "Well, at least he's holding."

The joke went flat. No one acknowledged it. They were just too down to look for any bright spot.

"Actually," said Drew in a more confident voice, "he's starting to close."

Casey was sticking with his plan. All of those long runs over cross country and indoor gave his legs strength. With about 150 to go he turned it up a gear and started moving up on Seacoast.

"Impossible," said The Deuce.

The team's new trainer JB was, if anything, a believer. A believer in anything River Hawks. He turned to the temporary coach and corrected him, "Anything is possible."

Halfway through the final turn Casey had waited long enough. Trailing Seacoast by two yards, he unleashed all of the speed he had left in his legs. Coming off the turn Casey moved out to the second lane and continued to run down the Seacoast runner, who was sputtering to the handoff.

His emotions swinging radically back to hopeful, The Deuce yelled, "Wow, what a run! It's all tied up!"

Lining up with the other anchor runners, Tooch watched Casey making ground on Seacoast. Shuffling around the other runners, he moved into position in the second lane next to the Seacoast anchor. The relay was coming down to his leg. With no lead on Seacoast, it was going to be a one-on-one duel for the win. For the whole season. The championship was now in his hands to win or lose.

For just an instant Tooch thought back to the conversation with his grandmother. People in his family were fighters and survivors. They had been through war, displacement, and emigration. His grandfather had led the way, taking care of his family in the hardest of times. Tooch was like his grandfather, he decided. He was going to face his fears, use his skills, and fight to win. Standing there in lane two ready to take the baton and run the race of his life, Tooch knew he would not fail.

"He can do it. He can do it," chattered The Deuce. He was a nervous wreck. The tension of the competition was getting to him. He needed reassurance. He grabbed Drew's arm and asked, "Can he do it?"

Normally Drew would have fed back The Deuce some positive energy, but something had just caught his eye. "I'm not sure," he said. The Seacoast relay anchor was Runner Ten. Although Drew had beaten him twice over the last few months, he had to admit that Runner Ten was talented. And the kid just won the two mile, which meant he was in shape. "Tooch is up against the two mile champion."

The two runners grabbed the batons and started off in a dead heat. Runner Ten had the inside on the first turn, and Tooch, who had paid the price of being boxed in earlier in the meet, decided to stay on Runner Ten's shoulder in lane 2.

Down the back stretch into the second turn the two runners ran side by side, shoulder to shoulder. Neither guy was giving an inch to the other. Even the slightest surge was matched by the other.

It was a gamble for Tooch to stay on the outside and not fold in behind Runner Ten on the turns. Running in the second lane for a 440 was a few yards longer than the first lane, and even if he matched Runner Ten's speed for the whole race, the additional few yards could tire him out and make the difference.

The Oaks was going crazy. Both teams were cheering and screaming for their runner. Except for the athletes near the high jump in the infield, every spectator was around the edge of the track adding to the noise.

Tooch and Runner Ten were rolling up on the next runner ahead of them as they ran down the straightaway to the 220 mark. Tooch made a quick surge to get a half stride lead on Runner Ten before they passed the fading runner. Runner Ten surged to match Tooch, but was running straight up on the runner in lane one, and had no room to pass. Tooch held his ground in lane two, passing the slower runner inches to his outside. Boxed in, Runner Ten had to decelerate, wait for Tooch to pass, then follow on the outside. Rounding the rest of the turn Tooch had a one stride lead and the inside lane.

The River Hawks exploded when Tooch took the lead. Jumping up and down along the back straightaway the girl's team screamed for Tooch.

Runner Ten didn't give up so easily. Once he hit the next straightaway he threw in a surge, caught up, and hung on Tooch's outside shoulder. The two runners were flying. His slow mile time earlier in the meet left Tooch's legs fresh for the relay, and he ran with the most power he ever had. Runner Ten, who had run the race of his life to win the two mile, was using all the strength he had left to anchor his team to victory. Heading into the final turn the two runners were rolling up on another runner.

"Don't get boxed in!" screamed Drew. If Runner Ten could force Tooch to slow down when passing the next runner, there wouldn't be enough distance left in the race for Tooch to recover. Drew yelled it again, but his voice was lost in the pandemonium.

Runner Ten made a slight surge to gain the advantage. This time, the runner they were coming up on sensed he was about to be passed and he wasn't giving up so easily. He accelerated, drifting to the outside of lane one, trying to make it harder for anyone to pass. Entering the turn, Tooch saw the gap between the rail and the runner and decided to squeeze through. Runner Ten, on the outside, swung out to lane three.

Three abreast, they rounded the turn. Tooch on the rail, a fading competitor in lane two, and high up on the banked track in lane three, Seacoast's Runner Ten. Running the shortest distance on the inside of the turn, Tooch had a one stride lead when the three hit the final straightaway.

It was down to the last fifty yards. Runner Ten, burning all the energy he had left, made an incredible surge, pushing himself past the runner in lane two and closed in on Tooch.

Tooch never looked back, his eyes focused on the finish line, now just ten yards away. He could sense someone coming up on him and assumed it was Seacoast's Runner Ten. He needed one more push, one more surge to hold on to the lead. Last fall during the XC season, Tooch had put in the long miles and built up his endurance. In winter, he had chased Aiken High's best miler through every workout and had sharpened his speed. Now, recovered from his head cold and fully rested, he was as fit and strong as he had ever been. He dug deep into his gut, found his last reserves of determination and pushed his body forward with all the strength in his soul.

Runner Ten, just about six inches behind, leaned to the finish line hoping to throw his chest across first, but his weak and wobbling legs lost balance, and Seacoast's best runner, the two mile champion, tumbled to the track short of the finish. Tooch, grimacing with determination also leaned, and with two more strong strides crossed the finish line ahead of Seacoast.

Two teams finished before Runner Ten could crawl across the finish line, and record Seacoast's final points. Gliding to a stop, Tooch bent over, put his hand on his knees and waited for the pain to flush away. He was lightheaded, nauseous and his body still throbbed, but he had never felt better in his life.

The River Hawks ran to embrace Tooch. Drew hobbled as fast as he could with his crutches. The girl's team ran straight across the infield.

"Hey! We're still here," Asher Dane sneered at the girls as they ran through the high jump runway. "How about some respect for the field events!"

Tooch, still breathing heavily and unable to speak, stood up straight and received high fives from his teammates. Theo Marshall grabbed Tooch around the waist and lifted his little teammate into the air.

Drew was closing in on the celebration when he was distracted by another argument between Stats and Gil.

"We have more points! Twenty-five to twenty-four!" shouted Stats. "What don't you understand about that? It's simple math."

Gil wasn't backing down. "But the total outstanding points don't add up," he said forcefully. "There's more points to be won."

"More points?" asked Stats incredulously. "Where? The races are done. The big man won the shot. Tooch came through. We've got twenty-five. They've got twenty-four. Where are the other points coming from?"

"Wait! What?" panted Tooch. He was still on Theo's shoulders. "Did we win or what?"

No one was sure. Drew racked his brain. He had watched all of the guys he trained with all season; sprinters, middle distance, distance, and even the shot put. Gil seemed so sure of himself, and it was hard to second guess the kid who worked the hardest to always be right. It all didn't make sense.

"Oh god," said The Deuce. He was the first one to figure it out. Pointing to the middle of the infield, he said, "It's the kid that sleeps on the mattress every afternoon."

Asher Dane, the high jumper, was calmly stretching out while waiting for his next jump. The high jump competition had run long and hadn't finished before the end of the relay. Seacoast also had good jumpers, and were likely to finish in the scoring.

"I didn't think about the high jump," admitted Stats.

Casey put it more pointedly: "No one thinks about the high jump."

They needed to know what place Asher was in, but Drew was afraid if they all charged over to ask the temperamental jumper, it might upset him. Asher didn't really fit in with anyone on the team and it was risky for just one of them to go and interrupt. Luckily there was now someone on the team that no one, not even Asher, could be bothered by. Drew turned to the team trainer and said, "JB, can you go over and ask Asher the score?"

"Oh yeah!" said JB. "I can get the score." He was very happy to get an important assignment. "I'll ask him. Asher will know. I'll just ask him the score. I'll find out. Sure."

The River Hawks all watched in silence as Asher and JB talked. "If that kid loses the meet for us," grumbled Theo, "I'll kill him."

"We'll all kill him," added Casey.

"No, no," corrected Drew. He had tried to get to know Asher over the season, and never completely understood the kid. But he was sure that threatening him wouldn't help. "That's just the opposite of what we need."

JB came back with the information. The bar was at six feet six inches and Asher was one of five guys still in the competition. He and a guy from Mayfield High School were down to their third and final jump to make it past the height. The Seacoast jumpers were already out of the competition.

Gil pumped his fist. "So, at worst, he's in fifth place," he said.

"That's four points for us," said Stats. "Twenty-nine to twenty-four. We win."

"No, wait! There's more," said JB. "Seacoast had two jumpers. Two guys. And they could jump! Six and Seven. Right behind us. Both of them."

"Sixth *and* seventh place?" asked Drew to be sure. He turned to Gil. "What's that mean?"

"It means they got five points when we got four," answered Gil.

"Twenty-nine to twenty-nine," said Stats, scrunching his face up in disgust. "A tie."

The Deuce whipped off his baseball hat and flung it to the ground. "A tie?" he asked incredulously. "That's just. . . just... " he was trying to find the word, "un-American!"

"So we would have to share the championship with Seacoast?" asked Tooch.

"Wait! There's more," JB said again. "Asher passed on 6'4.'"

"Passed? He didn't even try at 6'4"?" asked The Deuce. "Who the hell passes in a championship meet?"

There can often be jumpers who knock out at the same height, and to break the tie officials count up the number of missed attempts. The jumper with the fewest missed attempts wins the tiebreaker.

"It's not a bad strategy," said Drew. "He's gambling that if he ties at a height, he'll win on fewer misses."

"But if he misses at 6'6,'" continued Gil, "he drops to seventh place, and Seacoast moves up."

"Twenty-seven to thirty-one, Seacoast," said Stats dejectedly. "We lose by four."

The Deuce had lost track of what was going on. "Wait, you just said that we had twenty-nine. Now we could have twenty-seven? Why can't you guys play a sport where the score doesn't go down?"

"Look, it's pretty simple," said Drew. "If Asher clears 6'6" and the Mayfield High guy doesn't, we win. If the other guy clears, and Asher misses, we lose."

"Are you sure?" asked The Deuce. "This is it? The real, final decider?"

Gil and Stats looked at each other and nodded. Their calculations finally matched up. Turning back to The Deuce, Gil said, "All the points are accounted for."

"Yeah. This is really it," agreed Stats.

It was starting to get quiet in The Oaks Burdell Track and Community Center. For most teams the meet was over, and they had grabbed their bags and headed to the parking lot. Only teams with a jumper still in contention and the Seacoast Wave remained. The few lingering athletes rumbled out of the stands and crowded around the high jump runway.

Seacoast was rooting for the Mayfield jumper, since his victory over Asher would give their team the championship. The River Hawks had all their hopes on Asher Dane to clear the height and secure themselves the championship.

Of all the possible outcomes Drew had dreamed about, he never imagined it all coming down to the uncompetitive and fickle Asher Dane. While the other guys trained with intervals, long runs, and, for the throwers, weightlifting, Asher was often lying on the high jump mat with his eyes closed. "Visualization," he had called it. He once refused to attempt a jump for a personal record because he wanted to show "athletic collaboration rather than athletic competition."

Normally serene, peaceful and relaxed Asher started to look a bit uncomfortable as the crowds closed in on the runway. The high jump was not normally a heavily watched event, and he wasn't used to this many people watching his every move.

"He's looking scared," said Gil.

"He better be scared," growled Theo.

"What that boy needs," said The Deuce standing up straight and taking a step forward, "is a pep talk."

Drew held out a crutch in front of The Deuce. "No, no no. That's not what he needs to hear." Drew knew that threats, and a super jock rah-rah speech wouldn't motivate Asher. "Asher wants what we all want, to be part of something bigger than ourselves, to succeed, to be part of a team, to be respected and valued, to be..." He paused trying to find the right words. Whatever he was trying to say, Drew realized, should be said to Asher, and not the guys on the sideline. "I'll go talk to him."

The guys and The Deuce watched silently as Drew swung over and spoke to Asher. It was only a few moments, but with the balance of the meet in hand, every second seemed to last forever. At one point Drew reached out and put his hand on Asher's shoulder. Then before Drew returned to the team, the two teammates clasped hands.

"Is he all right?" asked The Deuce when Drew rejoined the team.

"Yeah. I think he's in the right mindset," answered Drew. "He's ready to perform."

"What did you tell him?" Tooch wanted to know.

"I told him that win or lose," said Drew looking straight ahead at the high jump pit, "we love him."

"What?" yelled Casey.

"No!" yelled Theo.

"Are you crazy?" yelled Stats. Then he took a moment to think about it. Drew always seemed to come up with the right thing to say when trying to win someone over. Looking at

Asher, now calm and collected, Stats had to wonder, "Do you think he bought it?"

Last night Drew's mother admonished him for not supporting his own brother and family, but with all that they had gone through together this season, he felt more connected to the guys on his team than anyone else in the world. The River Hawks indoor team were like his brothers. "I buy it," he said.

The Oaks became more quiet as the Mayfield jumper was called for his third and final jump. If he made it, there would be more pressure on Asher to match the height. The three teams, Mayfield, Seacoast and River Hawks quietly watched as he went through his pre-jump preparation. Casey reached over and put his hand over The Deuce's mouth to prevent another outburst.

With the crowd noiselessly watching his every move, the Mayfield jumper started toward the bar. He glided across the runway, curving into the center, then launched himself high over the bar, arching his back beautifully at the apex of the jump. But the heel of his trailing foot didn't snap up quickly enough and clipped the bar, tumbling it down with him as he landed on the mat.

Two teams let out an anguished groan. The River Hawks knew it wasn't cool to cheer for someone's miss, so they stifled their happiness as best they could.

"Next up," shouted the official, "Dane from Aiken. Third and final attempt at 6'6."''

Except for the buzzing of the ceiling light fixtures, there wasn't a sound to be heard. Everyone silently watched Asher walk to his mark and get set. He slowly rocked back and forth, looking at the bar, visualizing himself clearing the height.

If he missed, it would be a loss for the River Hawks. This was the final moment. A season worth of practice and training came down to a few inches of height. A championship team needs every member to perform at their best, and there was only one athlete left to perform.

Earlier in the season Asher told Drew that he considered the high jump to be an expression of beautiful athleticism, rather than competition. Drew had dismissed the idea at the time, but as he watched Asher's attempt he finally understood.

Crouched in a starting position and looking straight ahead Asher left his mark, gaining speed through the first three strides. On the sixth stride he began a smooth, arcing curve in toward the bar while tilting his body against the centrifugal force of the curve. Keeping his eyes focused on the top of the far standard he closed in on his takeoff mark. Planting his outside foot, he jumped straight up, thrusting his arms above his head. As the momentum of the approach pushed his body closer to the bar, Asher effortlessly rotated his shoulders so his face and chest were facing up toward the ceiling. With his arms stretched out above him he snapped his head back, causing his back to arch and clear the bar. In the instant his hips cleared, he tucked his chin into his chest, reversing the pivot point of the hips, and kicked his legs up high.

Asher's attempt was a combination of speed, power, body control, and perfect timing. It was athleticism in its most pure form. It was, Drew had to admit, a beautiful thing.

The jump and clearance had taken less than a second. Asher was, of course, the first to know, and he wore a smile as he enjoyed the clean ride down to the mat. He knew he was one of the guys now. He belonged on the team. A team of champions.

| 25 |

Drew's ankle took longer to recover than the doctor had predicted, probably because it was so hard for him to stay off it. When Asher had cleared the bar to win the championship, Drew tossed his crutches in the air and with the rest of the River Hawks, ran over to jump on the high jump mat. The adrenaline and excitement had kept him from feeling any pain on the run, but in the crush of bodies that piled onto Asher, someone, possibly Theo, landed hard on the ankle.

By the time the team jogged a victory lap with the trophy the ankle had swollen up to the size of a grapefruit, and Drew was having trouble putting any weight on it. The other guys were in celebration mode, laughing, slapping each other on the back, and retelling stories from the meet. The teasing Theo gave to Gil and Casey for dropping the baton was merciless. Stats and Gil still bickered about who had come up with the wrong tally going into the relay. Drew hobbled along with them, smiling, laughing, and wincing.

By Monday his ankle had been put in a hard cast and he had to thump around school slowly and gingerly. A week later he was still wearing the cast at the formal banner-raising ceremony in The Nest.

He had always imagined the banner raising would be a momentous and inspiring event, but he found it fairly anticlimactic. Since there was always a picture of the ceremony in the local newspaper, the whole thing was basically a photo-op for the adults. The principal, the athletic director, Mrs. Drain, and a few members of the local Rotary Club (they donated the money for the actual banner) lined up around Theo, Stats, and Drew. On one end of the banner was Coach Pilette, and on the other end was Coach Deuce, still wearing Theo's team jacket.

The cast was off and he was walking smoothly when they had the team party. Tooch's parents hosted both the boys and girls team at the family restaurant on a Saturday afternoon. Having never been in a Cambodian restaurant before, the guys were a bit awkward at first, but by the time Coach Pilette arrived with his wife and new baby, things got looser. The girls swarmed around the baby, and the guys started to joke around as usual.

The dinner at the restaurant was the last official team event, and the true end to the season. From here most of the guys would turn to their normal spring sports. Constantine and Traitor would move on to baseball. Both Stats and Theo were trying out for the newest sport at Aiken High, lacrosse. There was something about wearing a helmet and pads they couldn't resist.

Outdoor track never seemed to have the energy and excitement of indoor. Few guys ever signed up, and Aiken High's squad was perpetually short of point scorers. Drew never considered trying to recruit anyone. The only runners he was certain were continuing on to outdoor were Gil, Casey and Tooch.

Normally between seasons he would have organized some training runs with his core group, but his injury kept him from hitting the roads. When he was finally given the green light from his doctor to run again, he had to find a new running partner who would run at an easy pace with him. He didn't need a workout, just some casual miles to test the ankle and keep fit. There was one River Hawk who would be the perfect person to go running with, he felt, and he finally had the confidence to ask.

Mr. McKinnon sat at his kitchen table with his cup of coffee, trying to read the newspaper. It was his habit each night of brewing a new pot of coffee after dinner and letting the commotion of his wife and three daughters swirl around him. Shelley and Linda were working on a school project and, as usual, talking a mile a minute. At the same time, Mary and her mom were filling out an application for a summer camp.

When the phone rang the girls kept right on talking, and it was Mr. McKinnon, the only one not engrossed in conversation, who rose to answer the phone.

"Hello," he said over the din in the kitchen. After a pause listening to the caller he replied, "Well, hello, Drew. Congratulations on your great season."

The room fell silent. The three girls looked at their father, hanging on every word. Did he just say Drew was on the phone, they wondered? Drew Declan? It wasn't often a boy just called their house out of the blue.

Mr. McKinnon continued the phone call, "Oh, that's all right," he said warmly. "Records are made to be broken. I'm glad you were the one to do it." When Drew ran the fastest mile time in Aiken High history, it had been Mr. McKinnon's record he broke.

"What record?" whispered Shelley.

"Who is it?" whispered a confused Linda.

Mary rolled her eyes at her sisters' obliviousness.

"So, what can I help you with tonight?" Mr. McKinnon asked into the phone.

Shelley and Linda were starting to catch on to what was going on. They never had much of a conversation with Drew and they were surprised that he, of all the guys at school, would call their house. Neither girl had any interest in Drew, and weren't looking forward to talking to him on the phone. They looked at each other and at the exact same time whispered, "Is he calling me?"

Mr. McKinnon's eyebrow raised a bit as he listened to Drew, and then said, "Well, let me see if she is available." Turning to the kitchen table and wisely cupping his hand over the phone, he said, "Drew Declan is on the phone for you, Mary."

Shelley and Linda screamed, then started to laugh. Their little sister was getting a call from a boy. A senior, no less!

Mary's eyes had gone wide. She was just as surprised as her sisters. She jumped up, walked to the phone scowling back at her sisters, "Shut up! Shut up!" They would be teasing her about this for weeks.

Grabbing the phone and walking as far into the hallway as the phone cord allowed, Mary straightened up, turned her back to her sisters, and in a calm, almost nonchalant voice, said, "Hello, this is Mary."

That Sunday was the first truly warm day of spring. Snow from all the winter storms had melted from the walkways and lawns, and the remaining snow piles on the street corners were shrinking in the sun. The sidewalks glistened with thin puddles of the spring melt, and the edges of the streets still had a thin, gritty coat of road salt and sand. Here and there a branch of a maple tree was running with sap, and the sun sparkled through the falling drops.

Drew and Mary ran side by side along the Nantuc River. As he had hoped, the conversation was as easy as the pace. After all the worry about asking one of the McKinnons out on a date, it had turned out to be pretty easy. It just took him a while to find the right one. Linda or Shelley would never have gone on a running date, but to Mary, a real runner herself, it sounded like fun.

At around the two-mile mark his ankle finally loosened up and was feeling good. His strides were smooth and light and the distance they ran passed by effortlessly. Running was the best part of life and he was so happy to be back out on the roads again. There was a lot to look forward to, he thought. There would be races to win through the outdoor season, and plenty of workouts with the other guys. He might even be fully recovered by the end of the season, and take a run at another school record. And hopefully, there would be more days like this, running with Mary.

Drew Declan tilted his head back, looked at the perfectly clear blue sky above them and thought to himself, "My God, I love this."

A former high school and collegiate runner, Jim Ferguson still carries a passion and enthusiasm for running and racing with him when he hits the roads, track or trails.

Since 2006, Ferguson has been the senior colorist and on-line television editor for FRONTLINE, the PBS news and public affairs documentary series. Jim lives in Winchester Massachusetts with his son and daughter.

River Hawks Run is his first novel.